Two Boys Kissing

ALSO BY DAVID LEVITHAN

david levithan

two boys kissing

alfred a. knopf

new york

THIS IS A BORZOI BOOK PUBLISHED BY ALFRED A. KNOPF

All rights reserved. Published in the United States by Alfred A. Knopf, an imprint of Random House Children's Books, a division of Random House, Inc., New York.

Knopf, Borzoi Books, and the colophon are registered trademarks of Random House, Inc.

Visit us on the Web! randomhouse.com/teens

Educators and librarians, for a variety of teaching tools, visit us at RHTeachersLibrarians.com

Library of Congress Cataloging-in-Publication Data
Levithan, David.
Two boys kissing / David Levithan.—First edition.
p. cm.
Summary: A chorus of men who died of AIDS observes and yearns to help a cross-section of today's gay teens who navigate new love, long-term relationships, coming out, self-acceptance, and more in a society that has changed in many ways.
ISBN 978-0-307-93190-0 (trade)—ISBN 978-0-375-97112-9 (lib. bdg.)—
ISBN 978-0-307-97564-5 (ebook)—ISBN 978-0-307-93191-7 (tr. pbk.)
[1. Gays—Fiction. 2. Homosexuality—Fiction. 3. Love—Fiction. 4. Social change—Fiction.]
I. Title.
PZ7.L5798Two 2013
[Fic]—dc23
2012047089

The text of this book is set in 11.5-point Goudy Old Style.

Printed in the United States of America

August 2013

10 9 8 7 6 5 4 3 2 1

First Edition

For very different reasons,
this novel would not exist without

Robert Levithan,
Matty Daley,
and
Michael Cart

It is dedicated to the three of them.

You can't know what it is like for us now—you will always be one step behind.

Be thankful for that.

You can't know what it was like for us then—you will always be one step ahead.

Be thankful for that, too.

Trust us: There is a nearly perfect balance between the past and the future. As we become the distant past, you become a future few of us would have imagined.

It's hard to think of such things when you are busy dreaming or loving or screwing. The context falls away. We are a spirit-burden you carry, like that of your grandparents, or the friends from your childhood who at some point moved away. We try to make it as light a burden as possible. And at the same time, when we see you, we cannot help but think of ourselves. We were once the ones who were dreaming and loving and screwing. We were once the ones who were living, and then we were the ones who were dying. We sewed ourselves, a thread's width, into your history.

We were once like you, only our world wasn't like yours.

You have no idea how close to death you came. A generation or two earlier, you might be here with us.

We resent you. You astonish us.

It's 8:07 on a Friday night, and right now Neil Kim is thinking of us. He is fifteen, and he is walking over to his boyfriend Peter's house. They have been going out for a year, and Neil starts by thinking about how long this seems. From the beginning, everyone has been telling him it won't last. But now, even if it doesn't last forever, it feels like it has lasted long enough to be meaningful. Peter's parents treat Neil like a second son, and while Neil's own parents are still alternately confused and distressed, they haven't barred any of the doors.

Neil has two DVDs, two bottles of Diet Dr Pepper, cookie dough, and a book of poems in his backpack. This—and Peter—is all it takes for him to feel profoundly lucky. But luck, we've learned, is actually part of an invisible equation. Two blocks away from Peter's house, Neil gets a glimpse of this, and is struck by a feeling of deep, unnamed gratitude. He realizes that part of his good fortune is his place in history, and he thinks fleetingly of us, the ones who came before. We are not names or faces to him; we are an abstraction, a force. His gratitude is a rare thing—it is much more likely for a boy to feel thankful for the Diet Dr Pepper than he is to feel thankful for being healthy and alive, for being able to walk to his boyfriend's house at age fifteen without any doubt that this is the right thing to do.

He has no idea how beautiful he is as he walks up that path and rings that doorbell. He has no idea how beautiful the ordinary becomes once it disappears.

If you are a teenager now, it is unlikely that you knew us well. We are your shadow uncles, your angel godfathers, your mother's or your grandmother's best friend from college, the author of that book you found in the gay section of the library. We are characters in a Tony Kushner play, or names on a quilt that rarely gets taken out anymore. We are the ghosts of the remaining older generation. You know some of our songs.

We do not want to haunt you too somberly. We don't want our legacy to be *gravitas*. You wouldn't want to live your life like that, and you won't want to be remembered like that, either. Your mistake would be to find our commonality in our dying. The living part mattered more.

We taught you how to dance.

It's true. Look at Tariq Johnson on the dance floor. Seriously— look at him. Six feet three inches tall, one hundred eighty pounds, all of which can be converted by the right clothes and the right song into a mass of heedless joy. (The right hair helps, too.) He treats his body like it's made of fireworks, each one timed to the beat. Is he dancing alone or dancing with everyone in the room? Here's the secret: It doesn't matter. He traveled for two hours to get to the city, and when it's all over, it will take him over two hours to get home. But it's worth it. Freedom isn't just about voting and marrying and kissing on the street, although all of these things are important. Freedom is also about what you will allow yourself to do. We watch Tariq when he's sitting in Spanish class, sketching imaginary maps in his notebook. We watch Tariq when he's sitting in the cafeteria, stealing glances at older boys. We watch Tariq as he lays the clothes on his bed, creating the outline of the person he's going to be tonight. We spent years doing these things. And this was what we looked forward to, the thing that Tariq looks forward to. This liberation.

Music isn't much different now from what it was when we hit the dance floor. This means something. We found something universal. We bottled that desire, then released it into the airwaves. The sounds hit your body, and you move.

We are in those particles that send you. We are in that music.

Dance for us, Tariq.

Feel us there in your freedom.

It was an exquisite irony: Just when we stopped wanting to kill ourselves, we started to die. Just when we were feeling strength, it was taken from us.

This should not happen to you.

Adults can talk all they want about youth feeling invincible. Surely, some of us had that bravado. But there was also the dark inner voice telling us we were doomed. And then we were doomed. And then we weren't.

You should never feel doomed.

It is 8:43 on the same Friday night, and Cooper Riggs is nowhere. He's in his room, alone, and it feels like nowhere. He could be outside his room, surrounded by people, and it would still feel like nowhere. The world, in his eyes, is flat and dull. All sensation has been leaked from it, and instead its energy is running through the busy corridors of his mind, making angry, frustrated noise. He is sitting on his bed, and he is wrestling within himself, and ultimately the only thing he can think to do is go on the Internet, because life there is just as flat as real life, without the expectations of real life. He's only seventeen, but online he can be twenty-two, fifteen, twenty-seven. Whatever the other person wants him to be. He has fake profiles, fake photos, fake stats, and fake histories. The conversations are largely fake, too, full of flirtation he'll never deliver on, small sparks that will never turn to fire. He will not admit it, but he is actually looking for the surprise of something genuine. He opens seven sites at once, keeping his mind busy, tricking himself out of nowhere, even if it still feels like nowhere. He gets so lost in the search that nothing else seems to matter, and time becomes worthless, to be spent on worthless things.

* * *

We know that some of you are still scared. We know that some of you are still silent. Just because it's better now doesn't mean that it's always good.

Dreaming and loving and screwing. None of these are identities. Maybe when other people look at us, but not to ourselves. We are so much more complicated than that.

We wish we could offer you a creation myth, an exact reason why you are the way you are, why when you read this sentence, you will know it's about you. But we don't know how it began. We barely understood the time that we knew. We gather the things we learned, and they don't nearly add up to fill the space of a life.

You will miss the taste of Froot Loops.

You will miss the sound of traffic.

You will miss your back against his.

You will even miss him stealing the sheets.

Do not ignore these things.

We did not have the Internet, but we had a network. We did not have websites, but we had sites where we wove our web. You could see it most in the cities. Even someone as young as Cooper, as young as Tariq, could find it. Piers and coffee shops. Spots in the park, and bookstores where Wilde, Whitman, and Baldwin reigned as bastard kings. These were the safe harbors, even when we feared that being too open meant we were opening ourselves to attack. Our happiness had defiance, and our happiness had fear. Sometimes there was anonymity, and sometimes you were surrounded by friends and friends of friends. Either way, you were connected. By your desires. By your defiance. By the simple, complicated fact of who you were.

Outside of the cities, the connections were harder to see, the web thinner, the sites harder to find. But we were there. Even if we thought we were the only ones, we were there.

There are few things that can make us quite as happy as a gay prom.

Right now, 9:03 on that Friday night, we're in a town with the improbable name of Kindling—surely the pioneers had a fiery death wish, or maybe it was just a tribute to the burning sticks that kept the settlers alive. Somewhere along the way, someone must have learned the third little pig's lesson, since the community center is built entirely of bricks. It's a dull, quiet building in a dull, quiet town—its architecture as beautiful as the word *municipal*. It is an unlikely place for a blue-haired boy and a pink-haired boy to meet.

Kindling does not have enough gay kids to support a prom on its own. So tonight the cars drive in from far and wide. Some of the couples drive in together, laughing or fighting or sitting in their separate silences. Some of the boys drive in alone— they've snuck out of the house, or they're meeting friends at the community center, or they saw the listing online and decided at the last minute to go. There are boys in tuxedos, boys adorned with flowers, boys in torn hoodies, boys in ties as skinny as their jeans, boys in ironic taffeta gowns, boys in un-ironic taffeta gowns, boys in V-neck T-shirts, boys who feel awkward wearing dress shoes. And girls . . . girls wearing all these things, driving to the same place.

If we went to our proms, we went with girls. Some of us had a good time; some of us looked back years later and wondered how we had managed to be so oblivious about who we really were. A few of us managed to go with each other, with our best female friends covering as our dates. We were invited to this ritual, but only if we maintained the story line of our supervisors. It was more likely for Neil Armstrong to invite us to a prom on the moon than it was for us to go to a prom like the one being held in Kindling tonight.

When we were in high school, hair existed on the bland spectrum of black/brown/orange/blond/gray/white. But tonight in Kindling we have Ryan walking into the community center with his hair dyed a robin's-egg blue. Ten minutes later, Avery walks in with his hair the color of a Mary Kay Cadillac. Ryan's hair is spiked like the surface of a rocky ocean, while Avery's swoops gently over his eyes. Ryan is from Kindling and Avery is from Marigold, a town forty miles away. We can tell immediately that they've never met, and that they are going to.

We are not unanimous about the hair. Some of us think it is ridiculous to have blue hair or pink hair. Others of us wish we could go back and make our hair mimic the Jell-O our mothers would serve us in the afternoon.

We are rarely unanimous about anything. Some of us loved. Some of us couldn't. Some of us were loved. Some of us weren't. Some of us never understood what the fuss was about. Some of us wanted it so badly that we died trying. Some of us swear we died of heartbreak, not AIDS.

Ryan walks into the prom, and then Avery walks in ten minutes later. We know what's going to happen. We have witnessed this scene so many times before. We just don't know if it will work, or if it will last.

We think of the boys we kissed, the boys we screwed, the boys we loved, the boys who didn't love us back, the boys who were with us at the end, the boys who were with us beyond the end. Love is so painful, how could you ever wish it on anybody? And love is so essential, how could you ever stand in its way?

Ryan and Avery do not see us. They do not know us, or need us, or feel us in the room. They don't even see each other until about twenty minutes into the prom. Ryan sees Avery over the head of a thirteen-year-old boy in (it's true, so gay) rainbow suspenders. He spots Avery's hair first, then Avery. And Avery looks up at just that moment and sees the blue-haired boy glancing his way.

Some of us applaud. Others look away, because it hurts too much.

We always underestimated our own participation in magic. That is, we thought of magic as something that existed with or without us. But that's not true. Things are not magical because they've been conjured for us by some outside force. They are magical because we create them, and then deem them so. Ryan and Avery will say the first moment they spoke, the first moment they danced, was magical. But they were the ones—no one else, nothing else—who gave it the magic. We know. We were there. Ryan opened himself to it. Avery opened himself to it. And the act of opening was all they needed. *That* is the magic.

Focus in. The blue-haired boy leads. He smiles as he takes the pink-haired boy's hand. He feels what we know: The supernatural is natural, and wonderment can come from the most mundane movement, like a heartbeat or a glance. The pink-haired boy is scared, so incredibly scared—only the thing you've most wished for can scare you in that way. Hear their heartbeats. Listen close.

Now draw back. See the other kids on the dance floor. The comfortable misfits, the torn rebels, the fearful and the brave. Dancing or not dancing. Talking or not talking. But all in the same room, all in the same place, gathering together in a way they weren't allowed to do before.

Draw back farther. We are standing in the eaves.

Say hi if you see us.

Silence equals death, we'd say. And underneath that would be the assumption—the fear—that death equaled silence.

Sometimes you glimpse that horror. When someone close to you gets sick. When someone close to you gets sent to war. When someone close to you takes his or her own life.

Every day a new funeral. It was such a large part of our existence. Imagine being in a school where a student dies every day. Some of them your friends. Some of them just kids who happen to be in your class. You keep showing up, because you know you have to. You become the bearer of memory, and also the bearer of sorrow, until it is your turn to be the one who is gone, the one who is mourned.

You have no idea how fast things can change. You have no idea how suddenly years can pass and lives can end.

Ignorance is not bliss. Bliss is knowing the full meaning of what you have been given.

It is 10:45. Craig Cole and Harry Ramirez are planning their big kiss. There have been months of preparation leading to this kiss, and now here they are, the night before. Most kisses only require two people, but this one will end up needing at least a dozen. None of those other people are in the room right now. It's just Craig and Harry.

"Are we really going to do this?" Craig asks.

"We most certainly are," Harry replies.

They know they need their sleep. They know it's a big day tomorrow. They know there's no backing down, and also no guarantee that they'll make it.

They should be going to sleep, but good company is the enemy of sleep. We remember this feeling so acutely—the desire to linger away the hours with someone else, talking or holding or even just watching a movie. In those moments, the clock seems arbitrary, since you are setting your understanding of time to another, more personal measure.

They are at Harry's house. His parents are out for the night, the dog already asleep. Because the house feels theirs, the world feels theirs. Why would you want to close your eyes to that?

They are at Harry's house because Craig's parents can't know about the kiss. At some point they will. But not now. Not before it's happened.

Eventually Harry will leave Craig curled on the couch. He

will tuck Craig in, then tiptoe back to his own room. They will be in separate places, but they will have very similar dreams.

We miss the sensation of being tucked in, just as we miss the sensation of being that hovering angel, pulling the blanket over his shoulders, wishing him a sweet night. Those are the beds we want to remember.

We are excited for the kiss tomorrow. We don't see how they can do it, but we are hoping they will.

Pink-haired Avery was born a boy that the rest of the world saw as a girl. We can understand what that's like, to be seen as something that you are not. But for us it was easier to hide. For Avery, there is a thicker chain of biology to break. At a young age, his parents realized what was wrong. His mother thought that maybe she'd always known, which was why she'd chosen the name Avery—her father's name, which was going to be given to the baby whether it was a boy or a girl. With his parents' help and blessing, if not always comprehension, Avery charted a new life, was driven many miles—not to dance or drink, but to get the hormones that would set his body in the right direction. And it's worked. We look at Avery now and know it's worked, and appreciate the marvel of it. In our day he would have been trapped by an insurmountable body in an intractable world.

As they're dancing, Avery wonders if Ryan realizes, and worries that Ryan will care. The blue-haired boy sees him—this is for sure. But does he see everything, or only what he wants to be seeing? This is always one of the great questions of love.

Ryan is more worried by time, and what to do about time. He cannot believe he's found someone here in the bowels of the Kindling community center. The same place he learned to swim. The same place he took rec-league basketball when he was nine. The same place he's staffed bake sales and blood drives and the same place he'll vote, when he's old enough to vote. Yes, it's also the same place he ducked out of to have his first cigarette and, a couple of years later, his first joint, but it's never been somewhere he would have imagined finding a pink-haired boy to dance with. He can sense his friends watching from the sidelines, whispering about what will happen next. This only amplifies his own need to know. Time is running out, but what is it running toward? Should he stop and talk to this boy more, before the DJ plays the last song and the lights come back on? Or should they stay like this, paired by the music, cocooned in a song?

Talk to him, we want to say. Because, yes, time can be buoyed by wordlessness, but it needs to be anchored in words.

We know what their best chance is, and in this, the DJ does not disappoint. As most DJs will at some point in an evening, he spins a song that means a lot to him and nothing to anyone else present. Within seconds, the floor starts to clear. Conversations rise from a buzz to a clamor. A line forms at the men's room.

Both Avery and Ryan stop. Neither wants to leave if the other wants to stay.

Finally, Avery says, "I can't see any way to dance to this song," and Ryan says, "Do you want to get some water?"

An escape is made.

The DJ opens his eyes and sees what he's done. By all rights, he should switch the song. But it's a long-distance dedication to the boy he loves down in Texas. He dials up the boy right now and holds his phone into the air.

Not all songs need to be for dancing. There will always be the next song, to draw the dancers back.

This is what happens when you become very ill: Dancing stops being a reality and becomes a metaphor. More often than not, it is an unkind one. *I am dancing as fast as I can.* As if the disease is the fiddler who keeps playing faster and faster, and to lose step is to die. You try and try and try, until finally the fiddler wears you down.

This is not the kind of dancing you want to remember. You'll want to remember a slow song like Avery and Ryan's last dance. You'll want to remember dancing as Tariq remembers dancing, as he heads home from his night at the club. It's only eleven at night—which is barely noon when you're on party time—but he promised Craig and Harry that he'd get some sleep, so he can be with them for the big kiss tomorrow without nodding off. It was hard for him to step away from the music, from the pulse it created. He tries to simulate it now by blasting music in his ears, ignoring the other sounds on the late-night suburban train. It's not the same, because there are no other boys to look at or to be looked at by, just remnant commuters and some girls who've just seen some Broadway show. One of them tried to catch Tariq's eye earlier, and he just gave her a *nice try, sorry* smile, sending her back into her *Playbill*.

If you close your eyes, you can conjure a world. Tariq closes his eyes and sees butterflies. The vibrancy of them, spinning in the air to the music in his mind's eye. That's who he wants to be—on the dance floor and in life. A butterfly. Colorful and soaring.

There is something about the pureness of butterfly dreams, about all the things that dancing can unlock when you are young. When it works, that freedom doesn't stop when the last song is played. You take it with you. You use it for bigger things.

You notice when it's taken away.

Ryan and Avery can feel their words working with each other, can feel the simple joy of falling into the same rhythm, thinking companionable thoughts. Ryan's friend Alicia is giving him a ride home, and she is hovering on the periphery, shooting him a look every now and then. Ryan ignores this, because he and Avery are in their fortress of non-solitude, talking about how small their towns are and how strange it is to be at a gay prom. Ryan loves the way Avery's hair swoops, loves the shy curiosity in his eyes. Avery, meanwhile, keeps stealing peeks at the tip of Ryan's V-neck, at his jeans, at his perfect hands.

We remember what it was like to meet someone new. We remember what it was like to grant someone possibility. You look out from your own world and then you step into his, not really knowing what you'll find there, but hoping it will be something good. Both Ryan and Avery are doing this. You step into his world and you don't even realize your loneliness is missing.

You've left it behind, and you don't notice because you have no desire to turn back.

You keep your eye on him.

Perhaps because of the Diet Dr Pepper consumed earlier, Peter and Neil are up later than they expected to be. The date was a success, even though they've been together long enough that they don't even think of it as a date, just as a night together. They watched both movies in quick succession—horror first (for Neil), then romantic comedy (for Peter), with Neil holding himself back from smiling at Peter's fright during the horror and his tears as the romantic comedy resolved itself in predictable romantic comedy fashion. Peter is still self-conscious about these things, and Neil is conscious of this self-consciousness . . . even if he can't *always* contain his amusement. ("Are you all right?" he asked at a moment during the romantic comedy when Peter seemed particularly tense, and he couldn't help but squeeze Peter's arm with mock sympathy when Peter said, "I just want Emma Stone to be okay.")

Neither of their sets of parents are ready for sleepovers yet, so Neil left Peter's house a stroke before midnight, and now they are in their own rooms in their own houses, talking to each other over the Internet as they each get ready for bed. Every now and then one of Neil's Korean relatives pops up in the Skype column, and Neil is relieved that none of them attempt to say hi. Peter's connection is devoted solely to Neil, at least at this hour.

Peter thinks there is nothing more adorable in the whole universe than the sight of Neil in his pajamas. They are proper pajamas—striped button-down shirt with matching striped elastic-waisted bottoms. They are at least a size too big, and make him look like he's waiting for Mary Poppins to pop her head in and say it's time to go to bed. Peter is in boxers and a T-shirt that reads LEGALIZE GAY. Even though they've just spent hours talking, they spend another hour talking, sometimes sitting at their computers and looking at each other, and other times letting the cams gaze on as they walk around their rooms, brush their teeth, pick out clothes for tomorrow. We envy such intimacy.

There comes a point where Peter and Neil's conversation becomes too cloudy to continue. Even Diet Dr Pepper wears off after a while. But their cloudiness is the white, puffy kind, the kind of clouds that little children imagine will carry them off to sleep. Peter wishes Neil sweet dreams, and Neil wishes the same thing back. Then, for just a moment, they wave to each other. Smile. One last glimpse of pajamas, then goodnight.

Eventually, we all must go to sleep. This is our first intimation that the body always wins. No matter how happy we are, no matter how much we want our night to stretch out infinitely, sleep is inevitable. You might be able to dodge it for one giddy cycle, but the body's need will always return.

We used to fight it. Whether our allegiance was to talking in the dark or to dancing in the flashing lights, we wanted our nights to be endless. So the conversation could continue, so the dance could push on. We'd fill ourselves with coffee, with sugar, with stronger, more dangerous substances. But drowsiness would always tug at our tide, and eventually turn it.

We would playfully think of sleep as the enemy, the scourge. Why reside in the house of sleep when there was so much going on outside of it? And then the fight became more desperate. When you know you only have months left, days left, who wants to sleep? Only when the pain is too much. Only when you are desperate for the negation. Otherwise, sleep is time you've lost and are never getting back.

But what a pleasant negation it is. Drifting over the land of sleep and dreams, we can see why insomniacs beg and dreamers lead. We watch Craig curled on Harry's lime-green couch, under an afghan that Craig's great-grandmother crocheted. We watch Harry in his bedroom, his arms rounded and his hands beneath his head, his body a lowercase *q*. In another corner of the same town, Tariq has fallen asleep with headphones on, Icelandic music looping through his nighttime travels. In another town, Neil in his pajamas dreams that he and Peter are playing tic-tac-toe, while Peter in his T-shirt and boxers dreams that emperor penguins have taken over the local mall and are trying to sell sunglasses to Emma Stone. Back in a town called Marigold, Avery falls asleep with a phone number written on his hand, while in a town called Kindling, Ryan has taken a sleeping bag and has fallen asleep under the stars, smiling at the thought of a pink-haired boy and what they might do tomorrow.

Only Cooper is still awake, but that won't last long. He types himself into other time zones, talks with men who are just waking up, men who are sneaking a moment from work. He deceives them all, but cannot deceive himself. He is still nowhere, and no matter how hard he looks, there's no somewhere to be found, especially inside of himself. He believes the world is full of stupid, desperate people, and he can only feel stupid and desperate to spend so much time with them. We are worried by this. We tell him to go to sleep. Everything is better after sleep. But he can't hear us. He goes on and on. His eyes start to close more and more. *Go to bed, Cooper,* we whisper. *Go to your bed.*

He falls asleep at the computer. Men from other hours ask him if he's still there, if he's gone. Then they move on to newer windows, leaving Cooper's empty. He cannot notice when everyone else has left the room.

This is an incomplete picture. There are boys lying awake, hating themselves. There are boys screwing for the right reasons and boys screwing for the wrong ones. There are boys sleeping on benches and under bridges, and luckier unlucky boys sleeping in shelters, which feel like safety but not like home. There are boys so enraptured by love that they can't get their hearts to slow down enough to get some rest, and other boys so damaged by love that they can't stop picking at their pain. There are boys who clutch secrets at night in the same way they clutch denial in the day. There are boys who do not think of themselves at all when they dream. There are boys who will be woken in the night. There are boys who fall asleep with phones to their ears.

And men. There are men who do all of these things. And there are some men, fewer and fewer, who fall to bed and think of us. In their dreams, we are still by their side. In their nightmares, we are still dying. In the blurriness of night, they reach for us. They say our names in their sleep. To us, this is the most meaningful, most heartbreaking sound we ever had the privilege and misfortune to know. We whisper their names back to them. And in their dreams, maybe they hear.

We wish we could show you the world as it sleeps. Then you'd never have any doubt about how similar, how trusting, how astounding and vulnerable we all are.

We no longer sleep, and because we no longer sleep, we no longer dream. Instead we watch. We don't want to miss a thing.

You have become our dreaming.

In the middle of the night, Harry's mother opens his door, checks that he's safely asleep. Then she heads to the den and does the same for Craig, smiling to see him wrapped in the afghan. She knows they have a big day tomorrow, and she is worried for them. But she will only show her worry when they are asleep. Mostly she is proud. Pride is allowed to have an element of worry, especially when you are a mother.

Harry's mother tucks him in for a second time. She kisses him lightly on the forehead, then tiptoes from the room.

We miss our mothers. We understand them so much more now.

And those of us who had children miss our children. We watch them grow, with sadness and amazement and fear. We have stepped away, but not entirely away. They know this. They sense it. We are no longer here, but we are not yet gone. And we will be like that for the rest of their lives.

We watch, and they surprise us.

We watch, and they surpass us.

The music in Tariq's ears fades, the battery diminished. He doesn't notice. It is one of the body's greater gifts, the ability to prolong music long after it's faded from the air.

Asleep in his backyard, Ryan does not notice the halo of dew that gathers around him as the night warms into morning. His eyes will open to a sparkle on the grass.

* * *

The waking world. Even the most cynical among us must greet it with a touch of hope. Maybe it's a chemical reaction, our thoughts communing with the sunrise and creating that brief, intense faith in newness.

We fall quiet as we watch the sun reach over the horizon. No matter where we are, no matter who we're watching, we pause. Sometimes we look to the distance to see the dawning of the day. And other times we witness it as it's reflected on the people we've come to care about, watch as the light spreads over their sleeping features. How can you not hope as the world, for an instant, glows gold? We, who can no longer feel, still feel it, the memory is so strong.

Waking is hard, and waking is glorious. We watch as you stir, then as you stumble out of your beds. We know that gratitude is the last thing on your mind. But you should be grateful.

You've made it to another day.

Harry wakes up excited. Today is the day. After all the planning, after all the practice. This particular Saturday is no longer a square on the calendar. It is no longer a date talked about in future tense. It is a day, arriving like any other day, but not feeling like any day that has come before.

He goes straight from his bed to the kitchen—moppy hair askew, clothes sleepworn—and finds his parents there, gearing up in their way for his day. His dad is making breakfast and his mom is at the kitchen table, reading the crossword clues out loud so the puzzle can be filled in together.

"We were just about to wake you," his mother says.

Harry keeps walking to the den. Craig is sitting bolt upright on the couch, looking like the morning is a mathematical problem he needs to solve before he gets out of bed.

"Dad's making French toast," Harry says, knowing the addition of food to the equation will help it get solved faster.

Craig responds with something that sounds like "*Muh.*"

Harry pats him on the foot and heads back to the kitchen.

Tariq's alarm goes off, but he doesn't feel alarmed. With his headphones still dulling the outside noise, it sounds like there's music coming from the next room, and he takes it, slowly, as an invitation.

As soon as Neil is out of the shower, he texts Peter.

You up? he asks.

And the reply comes instantly:

For anything.

We smile at this, but then we look over to Cooper's house and we stop. He is still asleep at his desk, his face just barely glancing the keyboard, keeping the computer awake through the night. His father is coming into the room, and he doesn't look happy. All of Cooper's chat windows are still on the screen.

We shiver in recognition at what's about to happen. We

see it on his father's face. Who among us hasn't done what Cooper's just done? That one mistake. That stupid slip. The magazine left spread-eagled on the floor. The love notes hidden under the mattress, the most obvious place. The torn-out underwear ad folded into the dictionary, destined to fall out when the dictionary is opened. The doodles we should have burned. The writing of another boy's name, over and over, over and over. The clothes shoved in the back of our closet. The book by James Baldwin sitting on our shelf, wearing another book's jacket. Walt Whitman beneath our pillow. A snapshot of the boy we love, grinning, the conspiracy of us in his eyes. A snapshot of the boy we love who has no idea that we love him, captured oblivious, not knowing the camera was there. A snapshot we kept in our top desk drawer, in a fold in our wallet, in a pocket next to our heart. We should have remembered to take it out before throwing it in the laundry hamper. We should have known what would happen when our mother opened the drawer, looking for a pencil. *He's just a friend,* we'd argue. But if he was just a friend, why was he hidden, why were we so upset to have him discovered?

We want to wake Cooper up. We want to make the door louder as it opens. We want his father's footsteps to sound like thunder, but instead they sound like lightning. His father knows how to do this, his anger building quiet speed. He leans over his son and reads the remnants of last night's conversations. Some are merely conversational, a bored patois. *What's up? Not much. U? Not much.* But others are frank, sexual, explicit. *Here's what I'd do to you. Is that the way you want it?* We look closely, hoping for concern to spread over the father's face. Concern is okay. Concern is understandable. But we, who have looked so long for signs of concern in others, see only disgust. Revulsion.

"Wake up," the father says.

Anger. Rage.

When Cooper doesn't stir, he says it again and kicks Cooper's chair.

That does it.

Cooper jolts awake, his face pressing into the keyboard, creating an unsayable word. His contact lenses feel like dry wafers on his eyes. His breath tastes like morning worms.

His father kicks his chair again.

"Is this what you do?" is the angry accusation. "When we're asleep. Is this what you're up to?"

Cooper doesn't understand at first. Then he raises his head, swallows the meager spit in his mouth, sees the screen. Quickly, he closes the laptop. But it's too late.

"Is this what you do in my house? Is this what you do to your mother and me?"

From a cold distance, we know that confusion is at the heart of this disgust. And into that heart is pumping a steady flow of hate and ignorance.

We know that Cooper doesn't have a chance.

His father grabs him by the shirt and pulls him up, so he can be screamed at eye to eye.

"*What* are *you? How could you do this?*"

Cooper doesn't know. He doesn't know what to say. He doesn't know what to do. There aren't even answers.

The father's face is burning red now. "Do you just go off and fuck men? Is that it? While we're asleep, you go out and fuck them?"

"No," Cooper finally says. "No!"

"Then what is this?" A disgusted gesture to the closed computer. "What kind of whore are you?"

Fuck. Whore. These are not words any son should hear from his father. But the father's rage has its own language. It does not have to talk like a father.

"Stop," Cooper whispers, tears filling his eyes. "Just stop."

But there is no stopping. Cooper's father pushes him against the wall. Impact. The wall shakes and things fall. Cooper is no longer nowhere. He is somewhere now. And it is a horror. It is everything he never wanted to happen, and it's happening.

His mother comes running into the room. For a moment we are grateful. For a moment, we think it will stop. But the father doesn't care. He keeps yelling. *Faggot. Disgrace. Whore. Sick.*

"What's going on?" the mother yells. *"What's going on?"*

Cooper cannot stop crying, which makes his father even angrier. And now his father is explaining to his mother. "He sells himself to men on the Internet."

"No," Cooper says. "It's not like that at all."

"Open it," his father commands his mother. "Read."

Cooper actually lunges, tries to grab the laptop away. But his father knocks him back, pins him down as his mother opens the computer. The screen lights up. She begins to read.

"It's just chatting," Cooper tries to tell her. "Nothing ever happens."

But the look on her face as she reads . . . some of us have to turn away. We know that look. Something inside her is breaking. And in that breakage, she is giving up on us.

There is nothing more painful than watching someone give up on you. Especially if it's your mother.

Some mothers recover from this moment. Some never do. And within the moment, the trouble is: You can't know which way it will go.

"*You see*," the father says.

A fuse in Cooper finally reaches the explosive core, detonates. He has to stop this. He has to do something. He doesn't mean for it to be fighting back, although later it will look like fighting back. All he wants is for his mother to stop reading. So he jumps for the computer, tears it from her hands. In surprise, she recoils, and his father is too unprepared to catch him. But even though Cooper's gotten it out of her hands, it won't stay in his. He fumbles, and the laptop goes crashing to the floor, making a terrible sound. He reaches down and picks it up, but now his father is on him, pulling at his back, spinning him around. Cooper knows the blow is coming, and he lifts the laptop to block it. His father's fist is too fast, and it slams into his cheek before he can get the laptop up. "No!" his mother cries out. She gets in between them—she will do that much. Cooper doesn't hesitate. His keys and his phone are in his pocket. So he runs. He runs out of the room as his father rages behind him—raging at him, raging at his mother. He runs out the front door, runs to his car. He sees his parents coming after him, hears his father screaming but doesn't understand the words. When he turns the car on, the music blasts. He doesn't check to see if any cars are coming as he pulls out of the driveway, even though he knows this will only piss off his father more.

It only takes him ten seconds to leave his parents.

Besides strangers, they are now the only people in the world who know he's gay.

You spend so much time, so much effort, trying to hold yourself together.

And then everything falls apart anyway.

In the time it takes for all of this to happen, Tariq takes a shower. In the time it takes for all of this to happen, Craig (admittedly a slow eater) eats a piece of French toast. In the time it takes for all of this to happen, Peter loads up a video game and starts to play. In the time it takes for all of this to happen, Avery wakes to find a phone number still written on his hand, and wonders what to do next. He doesn't have to worry, though. Ryan is already on it. He has Avery's number in his phone, and as soon as the clock hits ten, he's going to call. He feels it's rude to call anyone before ten. So he waits. Impatiently, he waits.

It's funny the things you miss. Like phone cords.

Reading this today, you might not even know what a phone

cord is. Or it's a relic that you see in an office, or on that antique phone in the corner of the classroom, used to call the principal's secretary.

But once upon a time—that would be our time—a telephone cord seemed like nothing less than a lifeline. It was your attachment to the outside world and, even more than that, your attachment to the people you loved, or wanted to love, or tried to love. Everything about it was fitting—the way it curled in on itself, they way it got so easily tangled, the way you could pull it only so far before it kept you in place. Twisted and knotted and essential. It kept us tethered to each other, tethered to all the questions and some of the answers, tethered to the idea that we could be somewhere other than our rooms, our homes, our towns. We couldn't escape, but our voices could travel.

When the phone didn't ring, it mocked us.

When the phone rang, we clutched at it, grateful.

At precisely ten o'clock, Avery's phone rings. Avery doesn't recognize the number, then checks it against his hand.

"Hello?" he says.

"Hi," Ryan says, as happy to be heard as Avery is happy to hear him.

They begin to make plans, and a plan. Plans are the things you are going to do at a precise time, while a plan is the more general idea of all the things you might do together. Plans are the coordinates; a plan is the entire map. Plans are the things you can discuss in that first nervous phone call. A plan is the thing that goes unsaid, but puts the hope in your voice nonetheless.

While Avery and Ryan figure out what they are going to do today, the word *together* becomes the plan underlying the plans.

Avery knows his parents will give him the keys to the car again. So he volunteers to return to Kindling, to see what it has to offer. Ryan tells him it isn't very much, but Avery is experienced enough in his flirtations to say that as long as Ryan is there, it will be enough.

When Avery hangs up the phone, he smiles. When Ryan hangs up the phone, he panics. Buoyant objects still exert pressure. Ryan wants to clean his room, clean his hair, clean his life, clean his town all at once.

Avery, meanwhile, smiles his way to the shower. There are things for him to worry about, too, for sure. But those beasts are polite enough to wait at the gate until he makes his preparations.

There is nothing so heartening as a chance.

You will never forget what that feels like, that hope. Yes, we could talk to you for days on end about all the bad first dates. Those are stories. Funny stories. Awkward stories. Stories we love to share, because by sharing them, we get something out of the hour or two we wasted on the wrong person. But that's all bad first dates are: short stories. Good first dates are more than short stories. They are first chapters. On a good first date, everything is springtime.

And when a good first date becomes a good relationship, the springtime lingers. Even after it's over, there can be springtime.

* * *

A lot of thought has gone into the location of Craig and Harry's kiss.

If convenience had been the deciding factor, the obvious choice would have been to do it in Harry's house, or in his backyard. The Ramirezes would have been more than okay with this, and would have made all the arrangements that needed to be made. But Craig and Harry didn't want to hide it away. The meaning of this kiss would come from sharing it with other people.

It was Craig who suggested the lawn in front of their high school. It was public, but also familiar. The school itself was usually open on weekends for one reason or another—a football game, play practice, a debate tournament. But on the lawn, they wouldn't be in anyone's way. There was plenty of access to water and electricity. And their friends would know where to find them.

They debated over whether to ask permission. Harry's parents insisted on it. Harry and Craig made an appointment with the principal and explained their kiss to her.

She was sympathetic. Almost surprisingly so. She gave her permission, but warned them that there were still risks.

They accepted that.

Now here they are, pulling into the empty high school parking lot. Football won't happen until tomorrow, and play practice doesn't begin until two. The building has earned its indifference on this Saturday morning. It has seen many worse things than two boys kissing.

Smita, Craig's best friend, is already there waiting. She thinks Harry and Craig are crazy for doing this, and that of the two of them, Craig is the crazier one. Because, she thinks with only mild hyperbole, his parents are going to kill him. And if his parents don't, maybe kissing Harry will. Because when it all comes down to it, the breakup was much easier for Harry than it was for Craig. In Smita's eyes, Harry got off easy. He got to feel it was mutual. And then he got to go on with his life while Craig spent the next year still in love with him.

Okay, maybe not a full year. Smita isn't very good with relationship math. (Who is?) The point is, it was long enough. Too long. And even though Craig tells her up and down and back again that he's totally over Harry, that they're just friends now, and even though she's learned not to contradict him out loud, just to lay the groundwork so he can come to her later when he realizes he's wrong, Smita still thinks this whole plan is stupendously tone-deaf when it comes to what's really inside Craig's heart. We have heard her confess this to her sister, and her sister has been sympathetic.

Smita understands that there are bigger issues here, at least when it comes to the statement Harry and Craig are making. If you were to ask her under what possible circumstances would it be okay for Craig to kiss Harry again, she guesses this would be one of the few acceptable answers. She told them she thought it was crazy when they first told her about it (she thinks she was the first person they told, but really she was the second). And once they told her they were totally okay with it being crazy, what else could she say? She would always be on Craig's side, no matter what, and if that meant helping them research and fill out paperwork and plan for this absurd feat of political statement and potential heart-endangerment, so be it. With the precision of the doctor she will no doubt one day become, she worked with them to plot out the best possible strategy for maximum endurance. This meant countless hours of watching YouTube videos of people kissing for very long periods of time. It was the strangest homework she'd ever done. But her regular homework was already completed; what else did she have to do?

Now here she is, and here they are, and now it's closing in on the starting time. Once they start kissing, they will have to keep kissing for at least thirty-two hours, twelve minutes, and ten seconds. That is one second longer than the current world record for the longest-recorded kiss.

The reason they are all here is to break that record.

And the reason they want to break that record started with something that happened to Tariq.

We watch as he pulls into the parking lot. We watch as he sees them gathering—Harry and Craig, Mr. and Mrs. Ramirez. Smita, of course, and Rachel, who lives close enough to the school to walk. He sees them, but he doesn't get out of his car, not yet. Because one of the trickier qualities of the mind is its ability to be in two places at once. So Tariq sits there and at the same time he heads back to the worst night of his life. Factually, three months ago. Emotionally, yesterday and today and three months ago and any period of time in between.

Blood in his mouth. It is like there is still blood in his mouth.

The guys were drunk, there were five of them, and while it wasn't in this town, it was in a town close by. Tariq didn't have his license yet, didn't have a car. The movie was over, and he was waiting for his father to pick him up. His friends were heading out for pizza, but he had to get back. His father was running late, and the street became deserted once the end credits of the sidewalk conversations were over. There was someone in the movie theater booth, but that was it. Tariq couldn't stand still, so he walked a little down the block, to look in store windows. When the other guys started shouting, he didn't even know they were shouting at him. Ignoring them only made them pay more attention. By the time he understood what was happening, it was happening too fast.

He thought at first it was because he was black, but from all the variations of *faggot* they were throwing his way, he knew it wasn't only that. And some of them were black, too. He tried to walk past them, head back to the movie theater or even to the pizza place where his friends were, but they didn't like that. They boxed him in, and he felt the panic button being pressed. As they made fun of the color of his pants, as they taunted him some more, he tried to shove himself out. Threw his whole body into it, but there were too many of them, and they weren't caught by surprise. They shoved him back in and he tried to shove out again, and this time one guy hit him, a blow right to the chest, and as Tariq bent over, more guys joined in. Because once one guy starts, it's a game. Tariq fell to the ground, remembered someone telling him to curl up, to protect himself that way. They were laughing now, enjoying it, thrilled by it. He couldn't even yell for help, because the only sounds he could make were ones he'd never heard before, a wailing, gutteral acknowledgment of the sudden, intense pain as they punched and they kicked, laughing their *faggots* at him as they broke his ribs.

Across the street, someone saw. The woman behind the counter of the Thai restaurant came running out, yelling and waving a broom. The guys laughed at this—laughed at her broom, at her broken English. But then two of the busboys came out behind her, and they heard her yelling *police*. Tariq didn't see any of this, didn't even hear it. He was trying to get his vision straight, trying to curl further into himself, trying to spit the blood out of his mouth. As far as he knew, they were there, and then, with one last kick, they were gone.

His father pulled up a minute later. Found him. Took him to the emergency room before the police arrived.

As he bled on the pavement, pebbles and gravel grinding into his wounds, we felt ourselves bleeding, too. As his ribs broke, we could feel our ribs breaking. And as the thoughts returned to his mind, the memories returned to ours. That dehumanizing loss of safety. It is something all of us feared and many of us knew firsthand. We are not unfamiliar with what happens next with Tariq—the long healing, the surprising concern from some (including his parents) and the unsurprising lack of concern from others (like some, but not all, of the police).

The assailants covered their tracks well, and were never caught. We know who they are, of course. Two of them are haunted by what they did. Three of them are not.

Tariq is haunted, too, although mostly he is defiant. "They beat the shit out of me," he told people, soon after. "But you know what? I didn't need that shit inside of me. I'm glad it's gone."

He will not let it stop him from going into the city, from dancing. But still, the fear remains. The bruises. And there in the back of his mind, residing just as they did in the back of our minds, are the most insidious questions of all:

How did they spot me? How did they know?

What did I do wrong?

People like to say being gay isn't like skin color, isn't anything physical. They tell us we always have the option of hiding.

But if that's true, why do they always find us?

Cooper's loathing of everyone else—his parents, the people in his town, the men he chats with—is surpassed only by his loathing of himself. There is nothing that will add depth to despair like the feeling of deserving it. Cooper drives around, not knowing what to do, not knowing where to go. He barely notices that he's running low on gas. Then the warning light pops on, and he's almost grateful for it, because now at least there's a next thing to be done.

He wasn't always like this. Nobody is ever always like this. There was a time he was happy, a time that the world engaged him. Catching inchworms and naming each one. Blowing out candles on a cake his mother had made, with twenty of his fifth-grade friends around him. A home run in a pivotal Little League game that made him feel like a champion for weeks. A desire to draw, to paint. Shooting baskets at lunchtime with the other guys.

But high school confused things. He didn't want to do sports anymore. Friends moved away—if not from town, then from his lunch table. The dullness started to pervade the outside of his life, and the noise started to grow on the inside. He spent more and more time on the computer. This wasn't really a choice; it was simply the one thing that was always there.

Now his laptop is dead in the backseat. It doesn't really bother him.

In another car, Avery drives to Kindling. The land around him is flat, the horizon long. He tries not to rehearse what he's going to say to Ryan, because he doesn't want it to sound like a performance. All of the dates he's been on before have been half-hearted attempts with a boy in town who's known him way too long. Neither one of them was sure what he wanted, so they tried to put one another into that void. It never held, and Avery just happened to realize it five minutes before Jason did. "No harm, no foul," Jason had said, and this phrase in itself pointed to why Avery wasn't interested. He wants to be with someone who knows that a harm is much worse than a foul.

A boy with blue hair would have to know this, Avery thinks. Or at least there's a chance he knows this.

Avery is about to find out.

*　*　*

After a year, Peter and Neil feel they are beyond the discovery phase. But we're sure that they will continually discover this not to be the case. There's always something new to learn about the person you love.

Neil is not surprised to get to Peter's house and to find him still in his boxers, sitting on the floor of his rec room, navigating a fantasy world on his game console.

"I'm sorry," Peter says. "I've almost gotten the Guild of Wizards to sign my treaty. Twenty minutes, I swear."

Neil foolishly forgot his own homework, so he goes to Peter's room and fetches Peter's homework to do instead. It would be one thing if Peter's game involved massive amounts of battle and swordfightery. But from what Neil can tell, it's more about making and breaking alliances. In other words, politics, with beards and robes. Not his thing. *Balkan Bloodbath 12*, the game he brought over yesterday, sits on the ground.

Peter knows Neil's not into it, but can't help but play anyway. Because once this treaty is signed, he is going to be able to travel to the water nymphs' world for the first time.

He doesn't even notice what Neil's doing until he's through. Treaty accomplished, he finds that Neil is halfway through his English assignment.

"I can do that," Peter says. He knows he should like it when Neil does his homework for him, but he doesn't. He knows Neil does it because it's easier for him . . . and that's precisely why Peter doesn't like it.

"You have more important things to do," Neil says. "I mean, what's John Steinbeck compared to the fate of the Guild of Wizards?"

"I like Steinbeck."

"You know what would be cool?"

"What?"

"If your game took place underwater."

Peter knows Neil is going somewhere with this. Some joke. But he can't figure out the punch line.

He gives in and asks why.

"Because then the wizards could be fish, and it would be the Guild of Gilled Wizards."

Peter smirks. "I walked right into that one, didn't I?"

"More like you swam into it."

Peter likes these jokes, these jibes. Really, he does. It's just that he's not always in the mood for them. Sometimes he wishes he were dating someone a little stupider, or at least someone who doesn't think about each word in every sentence he utters.

Neil doesn't realize he's gone one step too smart. He doesn't change the subject because he senses something (slightly) wrong. Instead his innate gauging of the rhythm of the conversation knows it's time to move on.

"Pancakes," he says. "I think we need pancakes."

This time, Peter knows what's coming, and joins in. They both start jumping up and down on one leg, yelling, "I-hop! I-hop!"

We are such wonderful idiots, Peter thinks.

We often believe the truest measure of a relationship is the ability to lay ourselves bare. But there's something to be said for parading your plumage as well, finding truth as much in the silly as the severe.

Your humor is your compass and your shield. You can hone it into a weapon or you can pull its strands out to make your very own cotton-candy blanket. You can't exist on a diet of humor alone, but you can't exist on a diet without it, either.

All the quips in the world couldn't prevent Oscar Wilde from becoming a lovesick fool. But he rallied at the end. More than one of us borrowed his last words, staring off into the distance and uttering, "Either that wallpaper goes, or I do." There were even variations: "Either the mayor goes, or I do" or "Mother, either those shoes go, or I do" or "Honey, either that mustache goes, or I do." Maybe not our exact last words, and maybe not Oscar Wilde's exact last words, either. But you get the point. When the end comes, there will be important things to say, for sure. But there will also be that last laugh, and you will want it.

Laughter rarely lasts longer than a few seconds, it's true. But how enjoyable those few seconds are.

Before Harry and Craig begin their kiss, they are presented with some gag gifts.

Harry's parents present the two boys with a canister of Binaca. We laugh when it's clear that neither boy knows what it is. How would we explain it to them? That long ago, when you wanted your breath to be doused with mint, you'd pull out one of these slim metal tubes and spritz a little Binaca into your mouth. Whether you were covering up booze or covering up a more general sourness, you could rely on this hissing blast to do the trick. It didn't taste like anything natural, and if you were doing it before kissing someone, it always worked best if you both took a dose, so you could taste chemical together. In our arsenal of subterfuge, it was a largely harmless selection. We're amused by its presence now, in the same way that Mr. and Mrs. Ramirez are amused. After an explanation, Harry and Craig thank them, but neither of them tries the spray. They're chewing gum instead.

Their friend Rachel shows them that she's decorated a bed-pan with the face of an infamous radio talk-show host. They won't be able to use it during the kiss, but maybe right afterward. Smita takes out a bag of valentine hearts—not easy to find in the off-season—and shows them she's filled the whole bag with hearts that say KISS ME on them. Another friend, Mykal, has gone with another holiday and has attached a piece of mistletoe (also hard to find in the off-season) to the end of a fishing line, so he can dangle it over their heads as they kiss.

Finally, it's Tariq's turn. He's been setting up the cameras, making sure everything's been positioned right, so the lamps that illuminate the yard will also light Harry and Craig once night falls. If the kiss works, nobody's going to take their word for it. Everything needs to be documented precisely, so Tariq's got an army of cameras at the ready and a troop of reinforcement batteries on hand. Not only will the kiss be recorded, it will be streamed live, so no accusation can be made that the kiss was faked, or that any break was edited away. Three of the teachers from school have offered to take shifts as witnesses. Ms. Luna, the head of the math department, is starting.

But first Tariq has his gifts.

The first requires him to drag a duffel bag over the grass.

"Is that a body?" Harry asks.

"Or maybe just a head?" Craig wonders.

They are not far off. With a grin, Tariq lifts out a bust of Walt Whitman to preside over the event. Then, to mark the occasion, Tariq recites one of Whitman's poems:

> *We two boys together clinging,*
> *One the other never leaving,*
> *Up and down the roads going, North and South*
>   *excursions making,*
> *Power enjoying, elbows stretching, fingers clutching,*
> *Arm'd and fearless, eating, drinking, sleeping, loving,*
> *No law less than ourselves owning, sailing, soldiering,*
>   *thieving, threatening,*
> *Misers, menials, priests alarming, air breathing, water*
>   *drinking, on the turf or the sea-beach dancing,*
> *Cities wrenching, ease scorning, statutes mocking,*
>   *feebleness chasing,*
> *Fulfilling our foray.*

Everyone applauds.

Then Tariq breaks out his second gift—an iPod with exactly thirty-two hours, twelve minutes, and ten seconds of music on it, each song chosen and sequenced with the same care a DJ would use. All of Harry's and Craig's favorite songs are on there, as well as hundreds of other songs "donated" by friends.

"Just tell me when to hit play," Tariq says.

They are almost at the start.

* * *

In another town in the same state, Cooper realizes that a full tank of gas is only going to solve one of his problems, and a minor one at that.

He pulls into the parking lot of a Walmart. He takes out his phone and looks at the names in his contacts list. That's what they feel like to him—contacts. People he has contact with. Contact in class. Contact in the hallways or at lunch. Not friends. Not really. Not if being someone's friend means not being fake. He's been fake with all of them. Are there some who'd let him come over if he asked? Sure. Are there even some who would listen to what happened, who would worry on his behalf? Probably. But when he tries to play out that scene with any of them, it falls flat. It doesn't help. It only adds bystanders to what's essentially his burden, and his alone.

So he closes his contacts. He opens an app. He decides to talk to some strangers instead.

There are ten messages on his phone, too. He ignores them.

Avery arrives in Kindling, and his nerves crescendo. He remembers everything about Ryan, but doesn't really know much about him. What if last night was an aberration—what if, in the ordinary daylight of an ordinary day, the feeling of serendipity dissipates?

We called this *hopegoggling*. The fear that nighttime is really a rose-colored world, and that the morning will show that the things you hoped were happening weren't really happening, that your heart got ahead of itself. And, let's be honest, a lot of the time this was true—the force of loneliness was strong, and it swayed us. Or the euphoria of the helium hours was strong enough to lift us into the realm of improbability. The next day, the sugar rush had worn off. The next day, there was very little left to say to each other.

But sometimes—sometimes—it was there. The magic we'd created had remained. Maybe it even grew in the daylight. Because if it could be a part of our day, that meant it could be a part of our lives. And if it could be a part of our lives, it was a magic worth many risks and leaps.

We went through this so many times, but Avery has never felt like this before. He doesn't know yet that doubt lingers around anticipation like bees hover around flowers. The trick is to not let the doubt intimidate you into walking away. Doubt is an acceptable risk for happiness.

We count down the minutes until Avery pulls into Ryan's driveway. We count down the seconds until Ryan opens the door, comes stepping outside. Because we know that the best antidote for doubt is presence. Magic naturally fades over distance. But proximity—well, when it works, proximity amplifies magic.

The blue-haired boy smiles as he approaches the pink-haired boy. The pink-haired boy gets out of his car, finds the blue-haired boy waiting for him. They say their hellos. They teeter in an awkward moment. Then they teeter into a welcome hug, a reunion hug, a *this-means-something* hug.

Anticipation is no longer needed—because the moment is now.

* * *

Harry and Craig have taken their last proper bathroom breaks for the next thirty-two hours, twelve minutes, and ten seconds. The cameras are ready to go. Ms. Luna holds a stopwatch. Other friends have gathered. Harry's parents give the two boys two thumbs up.

It's time.

Harry leans over and whispers into Craig's ear.

"I love you."

And Craig leans over and whispers into Harry's ear.

"I love you, too."

Nobody hears them but us.

Then it's here. Months of preparation, weeks of practice, and years of living have led up to this moment.

They kiss.

Harry has kissed Craig so many times, but this is different from all of the kisses that have come before. At first there were the excited dating kisses, the kisses used to punctuate their liking of each other, the kisses that were both proof and engine of their desire. Then the more serious kisses, the *it's-getting-serious* kisses, followed by the relationship kisses—that variety pack, sometimes intense, sometimes resigned, sometimes playful, sometimes confused. Kisses that led to making out and kisses that led to saying goodbye. Kisses to mark territory, kisses meant only for private, kisses that lasted hours and kisses that were gone before they'd arrived. Kisses that said, *I know you.* Kisses that pleaded, *Come back to me.* Kisses that knew they weren't working. Or at least Harry's kisses knew

45

they weren't working. Craig's kisses still believed. So the kissing had to stop. Harry had to tell Craig. And it was bad, but not as bad as he feared. They had built a friendship strong enough to withstand the disappearance of kisses. It was off balance at first, for sure—their bodies not knowing what to do, the magnetism toward kissing still there, because even when the mind shuts off the romance, it sometimes takes a while for the body to get the message. But they made it through that, and they never stopped hugging, never abandoned all contact. Then Craig had this idea, and Harry wanted to do it. Enough time had gone by that when they started kissing again, the electricity was gone, replaced by something closer to architecture. They were kissing with a purpose, but the purpose wasn't them; it was the kiss itself. They weren't using the kiss to keep their love alive, but were using their friendship to keep the kiss alive. First for minutes. Then for hours. The hardest thing, when kissing for hours, was staying awake. Focusing. To be connected to someone else, but to be retreating entirely into yourself. Because when you kiss someone, you can't really see them. They become a blur. You must use touch as your touchstone, breath as your conversation. After many attempts, they found their rhythm. They made it to ten hours one Sunday. That was as far as they'd gotten. And now here they were, trying for more than three times as long. All to prove a point. And maybe it's all of the hours and maybe it's the point that's making this kiss much more intense than Harry had thought it would be. Their lips make contact and Harry feels a charge. It doesn't rise from the past as much as it's created in the present. Even though it isn't what they had planned, he finds himself putting his arm around Craig's waist, finds himself drawing Craig a little closer, kissing him a little more than the rehearsal kisses. The small crowd cheers for them, and Harry can feel Craig smile underneath their contact. He can feel that smile in Craig's breathing, in his lips, in his body. Harry wants to smile back, but is gripped by something more profound than a smile, something vast and inarticulate that fills his lungs, fills his head. He has no idea what he's gotten into, no idea what this all means. He thought he knew. He'd thought it out so many times. But what use is abstraction when it comes to a kiss? What use is planning? Harry kisses Craig and feels there is something bigger than the two of them just outside the kiss. He doesn't reach out to it—not yet. But he knows it's there. And that makes this unlike any other kiss they've ever shared before. Immediately, he knows this.

Craig is still thrown by the *I love you* that Harry whispered to him. That is what he's thinking about when the kiss begins.

Tariq makes sure all the cameras and the computers are working. He makes sure the live feed is working.

Right now, Tariq is the only viewer online.

* * *

We settle in. We watch.

Ryan doesn't invite Avery inside his house, and Avery doesn't ask why.

"Where are we headed?" Avery asks once they're both strapped into their seats. "What's the best Kindling has to offer?"

Ryan is torn. The Kindling Café is easily the best Kindling has to offer. But because of that, most of his school will be there on a Saturday, using the wi-fi and hanging out. If he takes Avery there, it will become a group event, and he doesn't want it to become a group event, not yet.

So there's only one destination that makes any kind of sense.

"The river," he tells Avery. "How do you feel about heading to the river?"

"I feel great about heading to the river," Avery replies.

Exactly what Ryan wants to hear.

One of the many horrible things about dying the way we died was the way it robbed us of the outdoor world and trapped us in the indoor world. For every one of us who was able to die peacefully on a deck chair, blanket pulled high, as the wind stirred his hair and the sun warmed his face, there were hundreds of us whose last glimpse of the world was white walls and metal machinery, the tease of a window, the inadequate flowers in a vase, elected representatives from the wilds we had lost. Our last breaths were of climate-controlled air. We died under ceilings.

Either the wallpaper goes, or I do.

It makes us more grateful now for rivers, more grateful for sky.

Avery figures they'll just sit by the river and talk. But Ryan has grander plans than that; he calls his aunt and asks if they can park in her yard and borrow her canoe. She says sure. So instead of heading by the river, they head right into it. It's a boat big enough for two—one in front, one in back. The current isn't very strong, and the space between the shores isn't very wide. They head upstream, not talking much, just a running commentary on the houses they pass, the shape of the clouds overhead. Then they get to a murmuring stretch, a shallow inlet.

"Here," Ryan says. "A drifting spot."

They put down their paddles, and Ryan turns his body so they're facing one another.

"Hi," he says.

"Hi," Avery says back.

"I would've brought fishing gear, but it's just so, well, mean to the fish."

"I'm a vegetarian."

"Me too."

A smile. "Of course you are."

Avery leans over a little, spreads his fingers in the water. It feels good to create a current, however small. The air is light and the water is quiet, the trees bending from the shore to listen to the tiny waves. The boat rocks gently.

"So what's your story?" Ryan asks.

Avery looks up at him, hand still in the water. "My story?"

"Yeah. Everybody has at least one."

For a few uncomfortable seconds, Avery worries that Ryan thinks he's a mutant, thinks he's a joke, and wants him to come clean. But then Avery realizes from Ryan's expression that, no, it isn't about that. Ryan is trying to craft a conversation, and wants it to be a meaningful one. Because what's more meaningful than a person's story?

"I can start if you want me to," Ryan volunteers.

"Sure," Avery says. "You start." Because it's a little safer that way. Avery doesn't know how he can tell *a* story without telling *the* story, and he wants to be sure Ryan was really looking for something that big when he asked his question.

"Okay," Ryan says. "Here goes." He takes in an endearingly nervous breath, then exhales the start of his story, telling Avery how almost everybody in his family was born here and how almost everybody in his family has stayed here. His father being the big exception. He left when Ryan was three, and Ryan and his mom were stuck for about five years after that, until she met his stepfather, Don. He's not that bad, as stepfathers go, but he's not what Ryan would've chosen, either. He's very old-fashioned about what men do and what women do. Ryan's mom is fine with that—she likes him being the boss. But Ryan's not as okay with it. They had two kids together, Ryan's half-sisters, Dina and Sharon.

"Dina's really sweet," Ryan says, "and Sharon is going to grow up to be a monster. She's only eight, but you can tell. If things don't go her way, the world has to pay for it, you know?"

Avery nods, and Ryan continues. "So yeah. That's the background. I grew up here, and I get into fights sometimes with my parents. My aunt Caitlin saves my life daily. Okay, that's an exaggeration. She saves my life *weekly*. She totally called it on me being gay. My mother was too lost in herself to notice, and Don didn't want to see it, so he ignored it. Caitlin waited for me to catch up to her. I had other things to think about at first—with Don, and then my sisters, and just fitting in to Kindling. Little League, that kind of thing. But eventually I noticed who I was staring at, and it wasn't the girls. I'll be honest—it freaked me out. I tried to like girls instead. I really did."

"How'd that work for you?" Avery asks, letting his voice joke a little.

Ryan mocks up a sigh. "Well . . . I went out with Tammy Goodwin for almost a year, in fourth grade. Really serious. I mean, we bought each other stuffed animals on Valentine's Day. That's practically marriage in fourth grade, right? By high school, I knew who I was. And when I told Caitlin, she wasn't shocked at all. She took me out on this river, in this canoe, and we'd talk about things. She's not a whole lot older than me— she's about to turn thirty—and she's had about as much luck with guys as I have. She's the one who convinced me I shouldn't try to hide. She said hiding never worked. She told me my dad spent so much time hiding that it was impossible for him to be happy here. He isn't gay—I guess that makes it sound like he's gay. He isn't. But he didn't want to stay here. He never wanted to stay here. He just wasn't strong enough to tell my mom until it was way too late."

Ryan goes on to explain he doesn't hear from his father much now. Just a phone call every now and then. Ryan visited him once in California, and it was a disaster. Ryan was twelve, but his father planned it out like he was seven. "He tried real hard, but in the wrong ways. He thought Disneyland could make everything better, you know? We ran out of things to say pretty quick. I emailed him when I was coming out to everyone, and his reaction was one of the best ones I got. He told me to do what I wanted to do. But part of me felt like it was easy for him to be okay with it because he'd given up on me a while ago. Like, he wasn't as invested as everyone else."

Ryan stops now, self-conscious the moment he steps out of the story. "Gosh," he says, "I'm talking a lot."

"No," Avery says. "Go on. How did everyone else react?"

"Oh, you know. Mom cried. A lot. Don was angry. Not at me, really. But at the manufacturer for giving him a defective stepson. My sisters, though, were fine. And so were most of my friends. I mean, a couple of them flailed a little in their first reactions—some of the guys were wondering if I was secretly in love with them. Which was only right in one case, but that went nowhere. The girls were by and large cool, even the churchy ones. Well, with one exception there, too. The inevitable rumors started, and I decided the only thing to do was confirm them, so I dyed my hair and started putting LGBT buttons on my bag and made noises about starting a GSA. The assholes in school had the typical asshole reactions. But there were a couple of other gay kids, so we banded together. I dated this one guy, Norris, for about two seconds, which was as long as it took for us to realize that the only thing we had in common was that we were gay. Our GSA advisor, Mr. Coolidge, is super cool, and has gotten a lot of things done, including the dance last night. That was his idea. The gay prom. We contacted every GSA in the area. Is that how you heard about it?"

"A friend linked me to the Facebook invite," Avery says. "Our GSA is kind of lame."

"Well, whatever got you there, I'm glad you made it. I guess that's the latest plot twist in my story, isn't it?"

Avery thinks it feels like a responsibility, to be a part of someone else's story. He knows Ryan is saying it playfully, not heavily. He knows Ryan is saying it to show that he's done with his own storytelling, which means it's time for Avery to start. Avery isn't sure that Ryan is a part of his own story yet, but that could be because he doesn't feel anyone can be a true part of his story until he or she hears it and accepts it.

They're drifting on the water—not much, just a gradual pull. Avery finds his mind drifting to a small part of Ryan's story, a small point of comparison. When he emerges from that brief thought, he sees that Ryan is watching him, waiting to see what he'll say next.

"I was just thinking about you and your aunt in this canoe," Avery explains. "How nice that must have been, to talk here. For me, it's always a kitchen-table war council. Us against the world. Coming up with a plan."

"That sounds stressful."

"Yeah, but at least everyone in my house is on the same side. I know how lucky I am about that. And unlucky in other ways."

"Unlucky how?" Ryan asks.

And this is it. This is where Avery must decide how much to tell, how much to let Ryan in. Like everyone else, Avery considers his inner world to be a scary, convoluted, inscrutable place. It is one thing to show someone your best, cleanest version. It's quite another to make him aware of your deeper, jagged self.

Here in the daylight, does Ryan already notice? Does he already know? If he does, it doesn't seem like he cares. Or maybe that's just more hoping on Avery's part.

Enough, Avery tells himself. *Just talk to him.*

The first sentence of the truth is always the hardest. Each of us had a first sentence, and most of us found the strength to say it out loud to someone who deserved to hear it. What we hoped, and what we found, was that the second sentence of the truth is always easier than the first, and the third sentence is even easier than that. Suddenly you are speaking the truth in paragraphs, in pages. The fear, the nervousness, is still there, but it is joined by a new confidence. All along, you've used the first sentence as a lock. But now you find that it's the key.

"I was born a boy in a girl's body," Avery begins. Then he stops, takes in Ryan's reaction. Which is surprise. His eyes widen a little. Then narrow as he takes a long look at Avery, figures it out. Avery feels like a body on display.

Or maybe Ryan is just waiting for the next sentence. "Go on," he says. His tone is encouraging.

"I think it was obvious to everyone from the start. And my parents are very . . . liberal, I guess. Practically hippies. So they actually tried to make it seem like I was normal. Or at least going through something normal. Now I can see the strain, and how much easier it would've been for all of us if I hadn't been born a girl. But they never made me freak out. It was everyone else. Well, not everyone. There were some people who were cool. But there were a lot of people who weren't cool. I was homeschooled a lot. We lived in a lot of towns, trying to find the right doctors. Eventually we found them, and I found other members of my tribe. Mostly online. But my parents and I go to conferences as well. They put me on hormones early, to sort of stop me from going through the wrong kind of puberty. Is this TMI? I'm sure you don't want all the details."

Ryan leans toward Avery, the boat rocking back and forth as he does. Avery grips the side, and Ryan puts his hand on top of Avery's.

"Tell me whatever you want to tell me," he says. "It's cool."

Avery shudders, and can feel the shudder travel through the boat, through the water, until the water becomes smooth again, until he feels his nerves become smooth enough to continue talking. It's too much, too soon, but now that he's talking, he can't stop. He's talking about hormones and the surgeries that have happened and the surgeries that are going to happen, and all along pretty much the only thing that's filling his head is the question of whether Ryan is seeing him as a girl or a boy. Now that Ryan knows, is Avery still a boy in his eyes?

Ryan is measuring his next words carefully—in fact, he's been weighing them, trying them out in his head, even as Avery's been talking. We don't blame him. We know it is sometimes hard to receive someone's truth. Not as hard as the telling, but still hard if you care about how your response will be taken.

Finally, he says, "I like whatever it is that makes you the person you are." It's like something his aunt Caitlin would have told him, back when he was figuring things out. Then, to show that he doesn't think this is the entirety of Avery's story, he asks, "Do you have any brothers or sisters?"

The conversation continues, and we leave them to have it. We watch from a distance as the boat drifts for nearly a mile, without either of them really noticing.

You can give words, but you can't take them. And when words are given and received, that is when they are shared. We remember what that was like. Words so real they were almost tangible. There are conversations you remember, for certain. But more than that, there is the sensation of conversation. You will remember that, even when the precise words begin to blur. How you gave, how you received. How close you felt to this other person, how remarkable this closeness was. The sharing of the words becomes as important as the words themselves. The sensation stays with you, attaches you to the world.

* * *

It was Craig's idea to kiss like this. And a half hour into it, he still doesn't understand what he was thinking.

There are many roots to it. One of them runs deep and connects directly to his childhood, to all those hours he spent poring over the *Guinness World Records,* dreaming that one day he'd be in it. The odder the record, the better—the world's largest cherry pie, or the man who could fit the most nails in his mouth. As a kid, he probably skipped over the kissing section. Too gross.

Then there's the root that runs closest, that runs right to where Tariq is standing with the cameras and the computer monitors, each one tethered to an extension cord they've run from the high school. Craig and Harry hadn't really been friends with Tariq, not before he was assaulted. Even though they were all out, they didn't move in the same circles. But when Craig and Harry heard he was in the hospital, heard what had happened, they felt the distance evaporate. Craig pictures him the day they visited his house, his body a badly matched collection of bruises, his usual smile too painful to use. Craig had cried—right there in Tariq's living room, he had cried, and he felt so awful about that. Tariq told him it was okay, everything was okay, they hadn't killed him. Ribs heal. Bruises fade. But Craig couldn't stop crying—not just because Tariq was hurt, but because it was so senseless, so enormously wrong. Harry tried to comfort him, and Tariq said more soothing words, and Craig wanted to feel *anger,* he wanted to feel raw outrage, but instead it was sadness that was filling him, an extreme, helpless sadness. He rallied then—stopped crying, let Tariq tell them what he wanted to tell. But for the next few weeks, the sadness wouldn't let go. At school he could distract himself from it, and with Harry and Tariq he could hide it. But when he was home it engulfed him. Because his family didn't know and couldn't know. They wouldn't beat him up. They wouldn't break his ribs. He knew that. But they had other ways of breaking him—with silence, with disappointment, with disapproval. His father would never accept who he was. Never. And his mother would go along with that. They had their beliefs, and those beliefs were stronger than any belief they had in him. Maybe this was the well that his sadness was being drawn from.

He knew what it was like to drown in it, to feel the sadness coming up to your neck, your mouth, your eyes. For a long time he thought he had a demon on his shoulders, weighing him down so he'd drown quicker. The demon liked boys, wanted nothing more than to kiss a boy. Craig couldn't get rid of him, no matter how much he wished it, no matter what promises he made to God. Then he met Harry, and suddenly the demon was revealed to be a friend. He offered Craig a hand, pulled him up. Craig emerged, gasping, from the sadness—then created a dam to keep it at bay. He didn't let Harry see it, just like he didn't let his parents see it. It had to remain inside of him, contained. When Harry broke up with him, the dam came undone. He started drowning again, even as he pretended for Harry and their friends that he could swim. Smita kept a close eye on him, and in his own way, Harry did, too. Their friendship helped him rebuild the dam. He still had his life within his house and his life outside his house, but he was almost used to that. It was all under control. Until he saw Tariq after the assault, and felt in his heart that this was his future, that this time the demons were as bad as he feared, and they were going to win.

He hated feeling this way. He hated feeling helpless. He wondered what he could do. How could he stand up for himself? He knew vengeance wasn't an option. He wasn't going to track down the guys who'd beaten up Tariq. He wasn't going to punish them. But there had to be some way to show the world that he was a human being, an equal human being.

He thought about protests. About gestures. About making the world watch. Then he thought about world records, and came up with the idea of the kiss.

There was nothing in the rules that prevented it. To the book of world records, a kiss was a kiss, no matter who was kissing. All the record keepers cared about was that the two people were standing the whole time, that there were no breaks, that lips were always touching lips.

The only hitch was that Craig couldn't do it alone, and he knew the only person he could do it with was Harry.

Harry had no hesitation. He thought it was a great idea. And when Craig and Harry told Tariq about it, it seemed to help him drown a little less, too. Harry was a dreamer, not a planner, so it was up to Craig and Smita and Tariq to figure out all the logistics. Craig was sure there were things they'd forgotten, and yet here they were. Here he was. Kissing Harry. Smita had been merciless in her teasing—*Surely, there are less elaborate ways of getting your ex to kiss you again*. But it wasn't about that. Or at least that's what Craig insisted to himself. It was Harry because they were the same height (no neck strain), because he and his parents were on board, because he took it seriously, because they had trained their bodies and their minds for it in a way that only two people who were really close could do. Harry's lips are so familiar to Craig. He has memorized these lips. And yet each time they were together was a little different, each time was a small thrill. These lips. Harry's arms around him. Their balance together. Craig could lose himself in this, if there weren't the need to keep it going for thirty-one more hours, if there weren't people watching, if it were about him and Harry, not about him, Harry, and the world. *Don't think of it as kissing him,* Smita said. *Think of it as standing for thirty-two hours with your lips together.* But how can he not think of it as kissing? He remembers the first time Harry kissed him, leaning over in the movie theater as the credits rolled. The surprise of it. The welcome surprise. The whole world narrowing down to that one intersection of skin and breath. Then expanding out, larger than before. A gasp of a kiss. His body remembers that. Even now. Even still. They have their signals—for water, for phone, for needing a squeeze, for calling the whole thing off. But there's no signal for what Craig is feeling. There is no way his hand can take the form of a question mark. He looks into Harry's eyes, wondering what Harry is thinking. Harry sees him, and Craig can feel his smile. But he still doesn't know what that means, or really what any of this means, except for the fact of doing it.

There are fewer than a hundred people watching them online—mostly Harry and Craig's friends, too lazy or too far to come see it in person. A few of those friends forward the link to other friends. *This you have to see,* they say. A few more tune in.

* * *

Two boys kissing. You know what this means.

For us, it was such a secret gesture. Secret because we were afraid. Secret because we were ashamed. Secret because it was a story that nobody was telling.

But what power it had. Whether we cloaked it in the guise of *You be the boy and I'll be the girl*, or whether we defiantly called it by its name, when we kissed, we knew how powerful it was. Our kisses were seismic. When seen by the wrong person, they could destroy us. When shared with the right person, they had the power of confirmation, the force of destiny.

If you put enough closets together, you have enough space for a room. If you put enough rooms together, you have space for a house. If you put enough houses together, you have space for a town, then a city, then a nation, then a world.

We knew the private power of our kisses. Then came the first time we were witnesses, the first time we saw it happen out in the open. For some of us, it was before we ourselves had ever been kissed. We fled our towns, came to the city, and there on the streets we saw two boys kissing for the first time. And the power now was the power of possibility. Over time, it wasn't just on the street or in the clubs or at the parties we threw. It was in the newspaper. On television. In movies. Every time we saw two boys kissing like that, the power grew. And now—oh, now. There are millions of kisses to be seen, millions of kisses only a click away. We are not talking about sex. We are talking about seeing two boys who love one another kiss one another. That has so much more power than sex. And even as it becomes commonplace, the power is still there. Every time two boys kiss, it opens up the world a little bit more. Your world. The world we left. The world we left you.

This is the power of a kiss:

It does not have the power to kill you. But it has the power to bring you to life.

Nobody is watching as Peter and Neil kiss. It is just a quick kiss as they leave the IHOP, before they head home. It is a syrupy kiss, a buttery kiss. It is a kiss with nothing to prove. They don't worry about who might see, who might pass by. They're not thinking about anyone but themselves, and even that feels like an afterthought. It is just a part of who they are together, something that they do.

Walking through the aisles of Walmart, Cooper isn't thinking about kissing. He is scrolling through his app, chatting with strangers, and kissing isn't on any of their minds. He came into the store because he was getting sick of the inside of his car, was feeling stupid just sitting there in the parking lot as moms and old people paraded in front of him with their shopping carts. Now he walks around as his mind is fragmented into screens and windows, torsos and come-ons, stats and entreaties. Most of the guys on here are older—some much older—than him. Cooper ignores the much older ones, but that still leaves him plenty to choose from.

"Hey, Cooper."

Cooper doesn't even recognize his name at first. This guy is telling him all the things he wants to do with his mouth, and all Cooper has to do is type *Yeah* and *Wow* and *Oh man* for the guy to go on.

"Cooper?"

It's the second time that gets through, and he looks up and sees this girl Sloan from school, looking at him weirdly. *Shit*, he thinks, shoving the phone into his pocket.

Sloan laughs. "You were pretty intense there. Don't let me interrupt you."

Cooper wonders what she saw. It was just a chat screen. No photos. She's not close enough to have read it, right?

"It's nothing," he mumbles.

"Oh, I know all about your secret life, Cooper."

Cooper feels like he's going to drop something, and he's not even holding anything. Sloan is in a few of his classes. Sometimes they're at the same lunch table. He never sees her outside of school. How could she know anything?

"You're an undercover Walmart cop, aren't you? Tracking delinquent teens like me. My eyeliner makes me a heavy shoplifting threat. I know the profiling that goes on here."

Cooper doesn't know what to say.

"I take your silence as complicity." Sloan puts up her hands. "Check my pockets if you must."

Why won't she just go away? Cooper's phone is vibrating like crazy in his pocket, and he imagines she can hear it every time it does.

She lets her hands fall. She's gotten the message that Cooper isn't playing along.

"But really," she says. "What are you up to?"

He really wants her to go away. He keeps his answer as short as possible.

"Shopping."

"For what?"

"Gas."

"Gas?"

He feels stupid. Why did he say that?

"For the grill."

"Because it's supposed to get warm tomorrow?"

"Sure."

This is the problem with having a barrier between you and everyone else—you see it, but they don't. They talk to you, but you can't talk back to them. They care about things like the weather and what you're shopping for, and you don't care about a single thing. It is so obvious to you, and it is infuriating that they don't understand. It just highlights that you're the one who's defective, you're the one who can't be normal, you're the one who has to suffer while everyone else gets to live out their delusions. We know. We've been there.

If Sloan were a friend, she would see something was wrong. If Sloan were a friend, she would feel comfortable asking what was wrong. But Sloan's not a friend. She's just a girl he knows. A contact. His phone is out of control in his pocket. Sloan looks at him funny. Then finally she says, "Okay, Mr. Social. I'll see you Monday. Good luck with the grill."

"See you Monday," Cooper says. He even tries to make it sound like he's looking forward to it. Because that will get rid of her faster.

The barrier still stands. Sloan moves on, and Cooper takes

the phone out of his pocket. These guys have barely realized he was gone. Cooper flicks through, still trying to find the guy he actually wants to meet.

All of these men and boys with their computers, all of these men and boys with their phones. All after the druglike rush of doing something adventurous, doing something they consider to be on the edge of something else. All of these men and boys fragmenting themselves, hoping the fragments are pieced together on the other end. All of these men and boys trying out this new form of gratification. All of these men and boys still lonely when the rush is over, and the devices are off, and they are alone with themselves again.

There is a term for this.

The term is *limbo*.

Better to be drifting in a canoe. Better to be brushing back your hair as it blows into your eyes. Better to know that everything you say is meant. Better to know that everything you say is heard.

Ryan asks Avery about the pink hair.

"I know, strange color choice, right? For a boy born as a girl who wants to be seen as a boy. But think about it—it just shows how arbitrary gender is. Pink is female—but why? Are girls any more pink than boys? Are boys any more blue than girls? It's something that has been sold to us, mostly so other things can be sold to us. My hair can be pink because I'm a boy. Yours can be blue because you're a girl. If you free yourself from all the stupid arbitrary shit that society controls us with, you feel more free, and if you feel more free, you can be happier."

"My hair's blue because I like blue," Ryan says.

"And mine is pink because I like pink. And I totally didn't mean to lecture you. It just makes me mad. All the stupid arbitrary shit."

"It makes you want to overthrow the world."

"On a daily basis."

Stupid arbitrary shit. We know what Avery means, and we also know he doesn't know the full weight of its harm, or the despair it can cause. He doesn't know how a single fact about a human being can mean that he and thousands of others like him will die, because nobody wants to talk about the disease that is killing them, nobody wants to spend the money so they won't die. *Stupid arbitrary shit* means the president of the United States can wait six years before even saying the disease's name. *Stupid arbitrary shit* means it will take a movie star to die and a hemophiliac teenager to die before ordinary people start to mobilize, start to feel that the disease needs to be stopped. Tens of thousands of people will die before drugs are made and drugs are approved. What a horrible feeling that is, to know that if the disease had primarily affected PTA presidents, or priests, or white teenage girls, the epidemic would have been ended years earlier, and tens of thousands, if not hundreds of thousands, of lives would have been saved. We did not choose our identity, but we were chosen to die by it. For stupid arbitrary reasons instilled by people who refused to see how arbitrary they were. We believe in the golden rule, but we also believe that people fail to live up to it, time and again. Because they fall prey to differences. Because some use the arbitrary very deliberately to keep their own power.

We don't burden Avery with this. Why would we want to? There is the hope that the world will get less stupid, less arbitrary, as time goes on. The good thing about human progress is that it tends to move in one direction, and even a fool who looks at the difference between a hundred years ago and now can see which direction that is. Moves like an arrow, feels like an equal sign.

In the meantime, we are vigilant. Deaths like ours teach you to be vigilant.

Avery looks at the river, looks at Ryan on the other side of the boat.

"The world from here isn't that bad, though," he says. "This right now is a world I can live in."

This is what the right people can do. They can make you see that better world.

There are things they aren't saying, of course. Ryan came down with such a severe eating disorder when he was thirteen, about the time he was coming out, that the school nurse made him get help. Even his parents don't know, because he swore the nurse and the counselor not to tell. And Avery isn't advertising the fact that he's never been past second base, and the idea of sex petrifies him. Ryan will not confide—not yet—his determination to head far, far away for college, and to never come back to Kindling again, not even for weddings or funerals. Avery will not detail the foolish lengths he went to get Freddy Dickson to like him, and how when it backfired spectacularly, he cut himself for the first and only time in his life. Not everything needs to be said at once. Sharing truth is not the kind of gift that comes in wrapping paper—ripped open once and, there, you're done. No, this is a gift that must be unfolded. It is enough to start the telling. It's enough to have the beginning and feel like it's a beginning.

Harry has been kissing Craig for forty-seven minutes, and he's amazed how easy it is. To be kissing Craig again, but without the drama of being boyfriends. It's so much more comfortable now. Much less fraught. He'd known all along that they'd get here, that they'd have this. When it was ending—when the boyfriend part was ending—he had been very deliberate about choosing his words. He didn't want to say *Let's just be friends* or *I hope we can stay friends*, because that made friendship sound like a consolation prize, the blue ribbon to look at distractedly while someone else walks off with the gold cup. No, what he said was: "I think you and I will be even closer, and that we will be even better together and more to each other if we're best friends, not boyfriends." He knows it still hurt Craig, and he knows it took some time for Craig to adjust, but he'd been right, hadn't he? They would have never attempted this if they'd been boyfriends. They would have never lasted long enough to get here. And he wouldn't have lasted even forty-five minutes if he'd wanted to do anything more than kiss Craig, if Craig turned him on anymore. Maybe there was something at the start, but now it's leveling off. He's glad Craig can't read his mind, because he knows it might be taken as harsh, but really it's a compliment. There are moments where Harry is so revved up, is so horny, that he'd sleep with just about anything. It takes a lot of restraint to realize the damage this can do, and to not venture places where you shouldn't go, even if you're revved up. He and Craig had fun, for sure, but it was never *about* sex. And now Harry needs to stop thinking about sex, because his body is starting to . . . react. So he thinks about something else—about whether he should ask for a sip of water. They're allowed to have some, but only if it's through a straw, and the lips are still touching. Tricky, but it can be done. The problem is, if he drinks now, he runs the risk of having to pee later. And he really wants to avoid that. This is another of the rules: no diapers, no cheating in the bathroom department. If he has to go, he's either got to whip it out and pee on the grass—or just leak a little into his pants. Neither option is really attractive, and the horny edge is totally off his mind now. Craig squeezes his arms, sensing that he's drifting off. Good call. He has to focus on the kiss. Not letting go of the kiss. The worst thing he can do is drift off. There are people all around, but he can't turn to look at any of them. He has to focus on Craig. And maybe the people over Craig's shoulder. That's it. He loves Craig, it's true. And the number one reason he doesn't want to mess this up is because he wants Craig to have this achievement. He wants to do this for Craig. Because it means more to him. Harry doesn't know why—maybe because it was Craig's idea, or maybe because he just needs something like this more. Yes, that must be it. Craig needs something like this more.

A small crowd is starting to form. People from town walking by, wondering what's going on at the school. Kids from play practice—some knew this would be happening, but others are learning about it for the first time. Mykal is organizing their friends and other people they know to get the word out, to get some cheering going. Some people—mostly adults—are curious enough to come over and look, then are disgusted when they find out what it is.

"Do their parents know?" one woman, walking her poodle, asks. "How could they let something like this happen?"

"His parents are right here," Mrs. Ramirez answers fiercely.

The woman shakes her head and walks away.

Other people—mostly kids—are asking how they can help. Lots of pictures are being taken on lots of phones.

One of the kids who asks to pitch in is eleven years old. His name is Max, and his dad brought him to see this.

Max is a marvel to us. He will never have to come out because he will have never been kept in. Even though he has a mom and a dad, they made sure from the beginning to tell him that it didn't have to be a mom and a dad. It could be a mom and a mom, a dad and a dad, just a mom, or just a dad. When Max's early affections became clear, he didn't think twice about them. He doesn't see it as defining him. It is just a part of his definition.

What does Max see when he looks at Harry and Craig? He sees two boys kissing. But it's not the two boys part that gives him pause. It's the kissing. He can't imagine ever wanting to kiss anyone for that long.

Just wait, we want to tell him. *Just you wait.*

After pancakes, Neil and Peter convince Peter's mom to drive them to the Clinton Bookshop. There are closer bookstores, but they're in the mood for a drive. Along the way, they don't say much, but their relationship has reached that stage where silence is comfortable, not threatening. Silence only harms when there are things that aren't being said, or when there's the fear that the well is empty and there's nothing left to say. Neither is the case here. They still have plenty to say to each other, just not anything right now.

At the bookstore, Neil looks for a doorstop biography to give his father for his birthday while Peter peruses the Young Adult section. It is there that Peter's phone buzzes, and he finds a message from his debate friend Simon. There's a link attached.

Peter takes a look, then tracks down Neil. "Want to see something awesome?" he asks, showing Neil the message, then clicking the link. "It's two boys in Millburn. They're trying to break the world record for kissing."

Neil looks at the grainy feed on the phone. "Do we know either of them?"

"I don't think so. But isn't that cool?"

Neil thinks it's cool. But his mind is stuck on something he doesn't think is cool at all.

"'Hey, beautiful'?" he asks.

Peter doesn't get it. "What?"

"That's how Simon started his text to you. 'Hey, beautiful.'"

"That's just the way Simon talks."

"I'm just making an observation."

"Riiiiiiiight."

"Don't dismiss me like that."

"Do we really have to have this conversation again?"

"Why don't you tell me, *beautiful*?"

"He's just a flirty friend. We both have flirty friends."

"Yeah, but mine are *female*."

"Clark? Clark is female?"

"Clark isn't flirty. He's too scientific to be flirty."

"He thinks lab partners should have full marriage rights."

"The only thing Clark has ever called beautiful in his life is an algebraic equation."

"Oh, but he'd love to see how his *x* corresponds to your *y*."

"Wait—how is this about Clark? I seem to recall it's about Simon."

"Simon is harmless."

"Simon is calling you beautiful and sending you a link to two guys kissing."

"Really? Of all the places to go, you're going to go *there*?"

They are a bit too loud. They don't notice the bookseller behind the counter, smiling. He knows firsthand that every relationship falls into this groove at some point.

Neil doesn't really think Peter is cheating on him. He doesn't think Peter would ever cheat on him. That's not what this is about. It's about Neil's fear that Peter will *want* to cheat on him, that he will someday realize there's someone better out there.

Peter is young enough to not really understand this. He thinks Neil is being foolish, slightly paranoid. He has done nothing wrong, and resents being attacked, anyway.

"Look," he says, "I think we need to step away for a sec. I'm going to go down the street and get coffee. Do you want anything?"

Neil shakes his head.

"Okay. I'll be back in a few minutes. Which is hopefully the amount of time it will take for you to realize that even if a million other guys say 'Hey, beautiful' to me, it doesn't change what we are, not one little bit."

"A million? Who said anything about *a million?*"

"There happen to be a lot of people who use 'Hey, beautiful' as a greeting when I am involved."

"Well, you are beautiful. I grant you that. It must be the *hey* I object to. It's so *common*. For horses, really. And you are so uncommonly, unhorsily beautiful."

Peter realizes this last twist in the conversation means things with Neil are curving back into being better, but now that he's mentioned coffee, he wants it. So he heads out, gets an iced latte, drinks it in a few gulps (too many damn ice cubes), then heads back to the bookstore. He finds Neil still in the YA section, his arms full of books.

"Wow," Peter says. "Are they putting you on bed rest or something?"

Neil puts the books on a table and shushes Peter with a finger to his lips.

Then he picks up the first book and holds it so Peter can read the title.

I Hadn't Meant to Tell You This

Peter quiets. Watches as Neil holds up the books one by one.

Just Listen
Stay
You're the One That I Want
So Much Closer
Where I Want to Be
The Difference Between You and Me
Positively
Matched
Perfect
Wonder
You Are Here
Where I Belong
I'll Be There
Along for the Ride
The Future of Us
Real Live Boyfriends
Keep Holding On

When Neil is through, Peter smiles and holds up his hand, gesturing Neil to wait there, to not say a word. He picks out two books from the YA section, then runs to the fiction section for a third. He is still smiling when he returns to Neil and shows his selections one by one.

Take a Bow
A Blind Man Can See How Much I Love You
Keep Holding On

Peter makes a stack of his books and takes a picture of the spines, to send to Neil. Neil then does the same for Peter. They put a few of the books back on the shelves and buy a few of them. (They'd buy them all, if only they had the money to do so.)

As they map their way in ribbons through the store, as they traverse the alphabetical and the topical and the arcane, we are reminded of bookstores where we went, of coffee shops and sex shops and Barneys and the Piggly Wiggly—all the aisles where we navigated relationships, all the conversations that were part of the aggregate conversation of our love.

It isn't until they're in the back of Peter's mom's car that Neil remembers the two boys kissing in Millburn. With his permission, Neil takes Peter's phone and clicks on the link again.

Neither one of them can believe it. Right there, in the town next to theirs, two boys kissing for hours in front of the high school.

"Not your typical Saturday," Peter says.

"No," Neil agrees. "Not at all."

Cooper had to leave Walmart after he bumped into Sloan, so now he's at a Starbucks a few towns away. It's full of people who are the same type of people who go to his high school and live in his town, but they're not the same people. Cooper feels anonymous, and that suits him fine.

He's flipping through three different hook-up apps, finding a lot of the same guys on each one. Forty-seven-year-olds who want him to come over. Eighteen-year-olds who want to flirt aimlessly. Twenty-nine-year-olds who want to know what he's into. He never starts the conversations. He never picks them out. It means more if they come to him, because that means he's desirable. And if he's desirable, he has the upper hand.

We think he is too young to know this. But he knows this. You learn it now at a much younger age.

By now, he's seen that there are at least a dozen messages on his phone, all from his parents. The house line. Each of their cell phones. He's not going to listen to them, and he's not going to call them back. He is blacking all that out. It is on the other side of the barrier. He doesn't know where he's going to sleep tonight, but it's not tonight yet, is it? He's sure some people would think it's denial, but it's not. He doesn't care. In order to be in denial, you have to in some way care.

All he feels is the bored emptiness of the flat, flat world. And there's no one who bores him more than himself. He looks again at the men on the apps, and this time a new one has popped up. Twenty-three. Hot. His screen name is Antimatter. His stats are the right stats. His one line of description is *Trying to find the sensible strain in the midst of all the chaos*.

Cooper waits for five minutes. He wants Antimatter to contact him first. But he's impatient. After five minutes, he thinks, *Fine*.

He goes ahead and makes the first move.

* * *

The question, in Avery's mind, is whether or not they'll kiss.

They've been on the boat for a couple of hours now. They've talked, they've paddled, they've talked some more. As the sun angles closer to the horizon, it's getting warmer. The canoe is metal, and it's becoming hot to the touch. They haven't brought anything to drink or eat, and the sun is starting to make them drowsy. Avery wishes the boat was wide enough for them to sit next to each other. It's so much easier to kiss when you're right there.

"I think I'm starting to bake," Ryan says. "Maybe we should go in."

Avery agrees. They start to paddle in earnest, and Avery is startled by the satisfaction he feels as he levers through the water, how gratifying it is to push through the resistance, to feel the effort in his arms. He is still a long way from being proud of his body, but sometimes a movement will catch him the right way.

The air cools as they move, but their bodies remain warm. They find their tandem and row in rhythm. Not a word needs to be said.

When they get back to the dock, they both have to wipe the sweat from their foreheads. Ryan jumps out first and ties down the bow. Then he holds out his hand to Avery. Even though he's an overheated mess, Avery takes it. Ryan pulls him onto the dock and keeps hold. They stand there, the canoe clanking against the dock in the slight tide.

"That was fun," the blue-haired boy says.

"It was," the pink-haired boy replies.

These words are inadequate.

Ryan keeps hold of Avery's hand as he ties down the stern.

Then he rises back up and turns their bodies so they're face to face, toe to toe.

"Hey!" a voice calls out—Ryan's aunt, coming down from the house. "How was the river?"

She walks a little closer, sees how they've moved a little bit apart, but are still holding hands. They're not looking at each other now; they're looking at her.

"So, Ryan," she says, "are you going to introduce me to your friend? I'm guessing you boys are thirsty. I have just the thing."

Just the thing.

Another hour has passed, and Harry and Craig remain in their kiss. More people gather. Mr. Nichol, a science teacher, takes over for Ms. Luna. There are now two thousand people on the live feed. Tariq hands Harry and Craig their phones, so they can tweet and respond to the comments on the feed. Already it's gone global. People in Germany are sending in encouragement; a boy in Helsinki has made a sign that reads GO KISSERS, GO! Some of the gay blogs have picked up on what's happening. Word is spreading.

Harry loves responding to the comments. But mostly he's concerned that his feet are starting to hurt, and it's only been four hours. He leans on Craig and shakes them out. Then the sun starts to hit, and he shapes his hand into a U, so Smita will come and hold an umbrella over his back, making sure not to get in the way of the camera. (There are backups from other angles, but everyone feels it's important that the primary feed should only be blocked in emergencies.) He and Craig are both wearing old-people socks, to try to keep the blood flowing in their feet. But the bottom line is that being upright for a long time is not how the body is supposed to work. Already he feels like he's at a standing-room-only concert and there have been seven opening acts.

The song "Dream a Little Dream of Me" comes on Tariq's playlist, which makes Harry think of the movie *Beautiful Thing*, as Tariq no doubt knew it would. Harry can feel Craig smile under his lips, and knows he must be sharing the same thought. As confirmation, Harry feels Craig's finger on his back, tracing the letter *B*, then *T*. They start to shuffle and slow-dance. It feels good to move their legs. Smita steps back with the umbrella, and Tariq steps in and starts to dance with her. Mr. and Mrs. Ramirez step in as well. Other people look like they want to join in, but Rachel, watching the cameras, tells them they need to keep clear, not get in the way. The police officer who's been assigned to watch over things offers to get some caution tape—Rachel says that might be a good idea, but asks if there's any way it can avoid saying *caution*. The officer says she'll see what she can do.

It feels so good to Harry to be dancing. It makes him so happy to see his parents smiling as they sway. He wants to sing along, but knows he can't. He holds Craig lightly, and they glide in a slow circle. Craig's eyes are closed, Harry's are opened.

Which is how Harry sees her first.

Craig feels Harry stop. He feels Harry clasp him tighter. He traces a question mark on Harry's back. But there's no way for

Harry to respond. He only kisses Craig closer, puts his hand on the back of Craig's neck, warning him to stay focused, warning him not to turn.

Then Craig hears it. His name. His mother's voice. His name.

We all turn to her. She is a small woman, who until ten minutes ago thought Craig was on a camping trip for the weekend. She looks more confused than angry, and we wish there were a way that we could explain it to her. We want to pull her aside and tell her everything we know, everything our mothers did wrong, everything our mothers did right. *Your son is alive*, we want to tell her. *Your son is living.*

She doesn't understand why he isn't answering. She doesn't understand why he goes on kissing this other boy even though she is standing right behind him, saying his name.

"Mrs. Meehan called me and started to talk to me, and I had no idea what she was talking about. . . ."

Craig wants to turn around. He wants to try to explain. But he feels Harry's hand on the back of his neck. He remembers why he's here. They are already too far along. He can't reset it.

"*Craig.*"

His mother's voice is cracking.

It's Smita who steps forward. She lets go of the umbrella and walks over to Craig's mother.

"He can't say anything," she says. "They have to keep kissing."

Craig's mother knows Smita. She's known Smita for a long time. Smita is the only thing that makes sense to her now. It's only vaguely that she understands the crowd, understands the cameras.

"What's happening?" she asks, her voice the thinnest of lines.

This was not the way she was supposed to find out. Craig feels the tears starting in his eyes. He tries to stop them. But it's too much. They leak down his cheeks. Harry holds on. Craig shudders, and Harry presses his mouth closer. This was not how it was supposed to be. He'd imagined telling them after. Somehow, he believed it could be kept a secret until it was over. He'd have this big accomplishment, and then he could tell them. He imagined gathering them in the den, sitting his parents and his brothers down on the couch while he stood in front of them and told them, like when he was little and he'd put on one-man shows for them right before bed—and whatever happened, they wouldn't be able to take anything away from him, they wouldn't be able to erase anything he'd done.

But he wasn't thinking about them. About what it would be like to be in that audience. He realizes it with such shock. He wasn't thinking about them at all. Few of us did. It was *our* revelation. *Our* event. How could we know that they had a right to feel things, too? They had no right to deny us. But they had every right to feel things.

He gets this all from the sound of her voice. The way she's said his name.

Harry's parents have never met Craig's parents. Harry's mother comes over to Craig's mother now and introduces herself. She and Smita try to tell her what's happening. They tell her about the world record. Tell her what Craig and Harry are trying to achieve.

"But I don't understand," Craig's mother says, crying now, too. "I don't understand."

Craig can't bear it. He opens his eyes, looks over to Tariq, who has tears in his own eyes. He mimes writing. Tariq scrambles for a marker and some paper. He runs it over to Craig. All the things Craig has to say boil down to the essential. It's the thing that neither Smita nor Mrs. Ramirez can say. It's within everything they're saying, but they can't unfold it for Craig's mother, can't spell out the foundation.

I'M GAY, MOM. I'M GAY.

Craig rotates his and Harry's bodies so he's facing his mother. Then he holds up his shaky sign. He sees her eyes as she understands it. Then, quickly, he writes another sign.

I CAN'T STOP NOW. I'M SORRY.

He is not sorry for being gay, but he is endlessly sorry that this is how she's found out. Or maybe not *found out*—she doesn't seem entirely surprised by the revelation, only in the way it's being revealed. Only in the way it's being confirmed. She's asking Smita if this is Craig's boyfriend, and Smita, poor friend, doesn't know what the better answer is, so she goes with the truth and says, no, that's not what this is about. Harry and Craig are friends. They are kissing to show the world that it's okay for two boys to kiss.

Mr. Ramirez brings over a chair, so Craig's mother can sit down.

"It's a lot to process," he says.

At this point, some of our mothers would have laughed, would have said, *Understatement of the year.* Others would have said, *Fuck you,* and stormed away. Still others did exactly what

82

Craig's mother does now—falling silent, falling completely into the sound of her own thoughts, which can't be heard from the outside. Mrs. Ramirez tries to hold her hand, give her support. Craig's mother pulls her hand away.

Craig is twisting in place, a bystander to one of the most important moments of his life. Harry understands this and loosens his grip. *If you need to go, it's okay.* But what can Craig say? And if he lets go now, all of this will have been for nothing. He lets the paper and marker fall to the grass. He wraps his arms around Harry and pulls him in for a real kiss, a true kiss. His tears run down his cheeks, into their mouths.

Don't let go.

The crowd cheers. Craig and Harry had forgotten they were there.

Tariq can't stand it. He feels it's in some way his fault, too.

He plants himself right there in front of Craig's mother and says, "You need to love him. I don't care who you thought he was, or who you want him to be, you need to love him exactly as he is because your son is a remarkable human being. You have to understand that."

And Craig's mother whispers back, "I know. *I know.*"

This time it's Smita who takes her hand, and she doesn't pull away.

"It's okay," Smita says. "He's fine. Everything's fine."

Harry can feel Craig going slack, and catches him. All that tension, suddenly released in sobs. Harry keeps his mouth on top of Craig's.

They do not break the kiss.

* * *

83

Some of our parents were always on our side. Some of our parents chose to banish us rather than see us for who we were. And some of our parents, when they found out we were sick, stopped being dragons and became dragonslayers instead. Sometimes that's what it takes—the final battle. But it should take much, much less than that.

For fourteen minutes, she sits in the chair. Watching her son. Watching her son kiss this other boy. Smita does not leave her side, but she doesn't try to talk to her, either. She lets her take it in. Lets her feel it through.

At first Craig can't face his mother. He and Harry stand so that she is seeing their profiles, out of their sight lines. But eventually he has to see her. So he shifts them around, dances a quarter turn, and looks at her over Harry's shoulder. Their eyes meet, and hold for a few seconds as Craig forgets to breathe. They both start crying again, but it doesn't seem as desperate as before, as devastating.

There are all these moments you don't think you will survive. And then you survive.

There are so many things Harry wants to say to Craig. All of the comforting words that gather on the inside of his mouth but must remain unsaid. We know how he feels, because we gather those words inside us every single day, knowing what we know now, seeing what we see now. But at least Harry can hold him. At least Harry can give him strength that way. And then he realizes there's another thing he can do. He makes the sign for *phone*, and then, after Tariq has given him his phone, he makes the gesture for *phone* again and points to Craig. Tariq is confused, but Rachel understands. She brings Craig's phone over to him and opens it to the message page.

Over his shoulder, Harry texts him.

It's better this way. It's going to be okay.

Craig texts back:

I think I know that. But it's hard.

Harry knows the answer, but he has to ask, anyway.

Do you want to stop and talk to her?

Craig shakes his head slightly, their lips still touching.

No. We're going to do this.

Meanwhile, Harry's mother has brought her own phone over to show Craig's mother the thousands of comments that have been left in support of Harry and Craig so far. There are close to four thousand people watching, cheering them on.

"I know you don't know me," Harry's mother tells her, "but we definitely have something in common."

This time when she offers her hand, Craig's mother holds it, squeezes it once before letting go.

It is hard to stop seeing your son as a son and to start seeing him as a human being.

It is hard to stop seeing your parents as parents and to start seeing them as human beings.

It's a two-sided transition, and very few people manage it gracefully.

*   *   *

It's sometimes easier with aunts.

Ryan's aunt Caitlin gives Avery and Ryan some pink lemonade and some freshly baked oatmeal raisin cookies. Countless times, Ryan has sat at this kitchen table when the world has felt like too much for him, when he's wanted to sit inside a house that fully felt like a home. We've all done this—created our mix-and-match families, our homemade safety nets. This table, he thinks, has seen so much of his anguish. But now, with Avery, it's witnessing the opposite of anguish. The table's presence makes it more real, because it makes it more a part of Ryan's life.

Caitlin is the girl we would've let ourselves be paired with, if we were going to be paired with a girl. After years of trying to rise in the world of corporate insurance, she quit and is now going for her library degree. Her sense of humor is indistinguishable from her sense of self. And her love for Ryan is the most unconditional love he will ever feel. It is unfreighted by expectations, untempered by motives. All she has to do is like him, and love him, and both are things she does well. Her responsibility to him is completely voluntary, and that's what makes it matter.

Avery wants to make a good impression, and is too nervous to realize this won't be hard. When Caitlin asks how they met, he turns it into the longest story in the history of humankind, telling her everything short of the amount of gas that was left in his tank after the drive home to Marigold. Halfway through, he knows he's talking too much, but Ryan and Caitlin don't seem to notice it as much as he does, so he goes on. When it's over, Caitlin asks, "And this was how many weeks ago?" It's Ryan who smiles and says, "This was all last night."

"It makes sense," Caitlin says. "With some people, the minute you start talking, it feels like you've known them for years. It only means that you were supposed to meet sooner. You're feeling all the time you should've known each other, but didn't. That time still counts. You can definitely feel it."

Avery knows he should be trying to get Ryan away, should be trying to get him alone, get him close enough to kiss. Time is quietly ticking down to the moment he'll have to leave—he promised his mother he'd be home before dark. But he is enjoying the company, the lemonade, the cookies. He feels it's probably wrong to think of this as more worthy than kissing and making out. But right now, it is.

"Do you want to see some embarrassing photos of Ryan dressed up as Britney Spears for Halloween?" Caitlin asks.

How can Avery say no?

Meanwhile, Cooper has been chatting with Antimatter for almost an hour. As far as Antimatter knows, Cooper is a nineteen-year-old student at the local county college. He's majoring in finance and has two roommates, one of whom is a drunk. Antimatter doesn't question this, and says that he's just gotten his own place and is working as the manager of a coffee shop. He's a painter, too, but there hasn't been much money in that so far. Cooper used to want to be a painter, and finds himself telling

Antimatter this. Antimatter asks what happened, and Cooper says he lost interest. *Story of my life*, Cooper tells him. Antimatter responds, *Story isn't over yet.*

Cooper is a little interested and a little bored. To up the ante, he sends a shirtless pic to Antimatter, and Antimatter responds in kind. He's got a great body. Cooper asks him if he wants to meet up. Antimatter says sure—maybe after dinner? Cooper wonders what dinner plans Antimatter has, but doesn't ask. He just says that'd be fine. He suggests the Starbucks he's sitting in. Antimatter says that will work, as long as they don't have to drink the coffee. Cooper, who's already had three, is okay with that.

Now that the date is set, Antimatter says he probably should go do some IRL things.

But before I go . . . what's your name?

Drake, Cooper answers.

Hi, Drake. I'm Julian.

Cooper can't help it—he liked him better as Antimatter.

But he doesn't cancel the meet-up. It would be stupid to cancel over something as dumb as a name.

When you have been dead as long as we have, you begin to see all the angles that existed in your life, especially the ones you were too blind to see at the time. You have plenty of time to chart the paths of your major and minor mistakes, and to have a newfound sympathy for the mistakes other people make. At times, we were helpless, it's true. But other times we were heartless. We screwed ourselves up, screwed other people over, said words we didn't know would hurt, said words precisely because we knew they would wound. Even after what we went through, no retroactive saintliness can be granted. We understand our fuck ups more now from a distance, but that doesn't make them any less real.

You must understand: We were like Cooper. Or at least we had moments when we were like Cooper. Just as we had moments when we were like Neil, Peter, Harry, Craig, Tariq, Avery, Ryan. We had moments when we were like each of you.

This is how we understand. We wore your flaws. We wore your fears. We made your mistakes.

Six hours and ten minutes into Harry and Craig's kiss, a popular blogger with hair an even brighter pink than Avery's posts about Harry and Craig and tells the world to get behind what they're doing.

The number of people viewing the kiss goes from 3,928 to 40,102 within five minutes, and then to 103,039 five minutes after that.

At the same time this is happening, Craig's mother stands up from her chair and walks over to him. She asks Smita if it's possible for her to remain off camera, and for the sound to be turned off while she is speaking to her son. Smita passes the request to Tariq, who obliges.

"I need to get back home," Craig's mother tells him. "Your father and your brothers will be home soon, and I should be there." She pauses. It is clear from his eyes that Craig is listening, even though he is kissing Harry at the same time. "I hope you realize that I am going to have to tell them what you are doing. If they find out from anyone else, it will be . . . worse. Do you understand?"

Craig wants to say yes, knows he could make his voice say "uh-huh" at the very least, but that doesn't feel right. The sign they agreed upon for yes is a thumbs-up, which also feels wrong. But Craig can't think of anything else. So he gives his mother a thumbs-up.

Craig's mother takes a deep breath. She is not finished. After she exhales she says, in a voice as level as she can manage, "I love you, Craig. I am also very angry at you. Not because you are gay. We will deal with that. But to find out this way . . . it's not what I would have wanted. I am sure you had your reasons, and I hope you will be willing to talk about them with us when this whole . . . thing is through."

Again, Craig gives his mother a thumbs-up. He feels ridiculous.

His mother's expression softens. "Do you need anything?" she asks.

For a moment, Craig's heart feels entirely porous. Not because his mother has asked such a monumental question, but because it's such an ordinary one. This is the mother he knows. *Do you need anything?* As if she were running to Walgreens or the grocery store. As if nothing has changed.

There is no way for Craig to say, *I need you to convince Dad and Sam and Kevin that this is fine. I need you to support me as much as Harry's parents support him. I need you to be proud of what I'm doing, because it will matter so much more if you are. I need you to come back. I need to know that neither of us is going to drown from this.*

His fingers make an okay sign.

"All right, then," she says. "I'll go."

He wants her to come over and hug him. Or at least put her hand on his shoulder.

But instead she turns and starts her walk home. Harry, sensing what's happening, starts to switch their positions, so Craig doesn't have to see her go. But Craig holds firm. He watches as she says goodbye to Smita—not to Harry's parents, not to anyone else, just to Smita—and then steps into the crowd. They all face forward, but she faces home. He watches as she becomes a small shape on the sidewalk, then moves out of his sight line. It is about a ten-minute walk home from here, and he's sure his heartbeat will count off the steps until she gets there. Then it will stop.

It is only after she is gone, only after he pictures her alone, walking, that his vision draws back closer. For the first time since she arrived, he realizes how thick the crowd has become. There are so many unfamiliar faces here, as well as familiar ones. Someone starts a chant—"Harry and Craig, All the Way! Harry and Craig, All the Way!" He knows he should be taking strength from this, that he should be encouraged. But the truth is, he has left his body for a little while. He is hovering over his house, too far up in the air to see his mother return, too human to see through the ceiling or hear through the wind how the conversation in his parents' bedroom goes.

* * *

Peter and Neil are in Peter's room, watching the live feed online.

"Was that his mother?" Peter asks.

"I think so," Neil says. "They cut in so fast, it was hard to tell. But I think it was."

"Do you think she knew about it ahead of time?"

"From the way she looked before, probably not." Neil can imagine his own mother looking the same way, and is trying not to think about that.

"How long do you think we could last?" Peter asks.

"Having a son like Craig? Pretty long, I think."

"Ha ha. I mean kissing."

"Not thirty-two hours. But a few hours."

"Here." Peter pulls Neil off his desk chair, stands him in the middle of the room. "Let's try."

"Right this moment?"

"No time like the present."

Before Neil can protest, Peter kisses him . . . and stays there. For the first minute or two, it feels totally normal—the tender pressure, tongues corresponding, hands tracing spines, gliding down hips. Then comes the moment in the rhythm when they would usually take a breath—smile or say something or pull back so fingers could trail down. They move through the pause, draw out their ardor. Peter lingers his hand down Neil's back, slips his fingers beneath his waistband, rests on the skin there, the heat. Neil moves in the opposite direction, his hand rising under the back of Peter's shirt, between his shoulder blades. Peter still tastes like coffee and milk; Neil tastes like winter mint. Peter's breath staggers a little in his lungs. Neil touches the nape of his neck, then slowly retreats back down, fingernails raking skin. They are hyperconscious of their bodies, hyperconscious of their breathing. Peter brings his hand around, lifts his palm to Neil's heartbeat. Minutes pass. Their bodies grow hotter. Their kiss is wetter. Peter's stubble presses prickly against Neil's chin. Peter feels the silence of the room, the lack of music. Their hips lock against each other. Neil's breath quickens. Peter's underwear grows tighter. Neither wants to be the one who pulls away. Eleven minutes. Twelve minutes. Peter loses track of his breathing, exhales when he should inhale. Instinctively, he pulls back for more breath, and just like that, the kiss is broken. The moment it breaks, Neil lets his arms fall. They step away from each other. They look at the clock.

"That was intense," Peter says, adjusting his jeans.

"Yeah," Neil says, wiping some saliva from his stubble-suffering chin.

They turn back to the screen, see Harry and Craig in their dance.

Peter is about to say something else, but his father calls up to say that dinner is ready, it's time to come down.

Avery can try to ignore the clock, but it's harder to ignore the sun. He and Ryan say goodbye to Caitlin, each of them giving her a hug and a kiss on the cheek. Avery's already called home, looking for an extension. But he's only had a license for a little while, and has never driven at night on the highway before. His mother doesn't want his first time to be alone, and it's hard to argue with that. But he will push dusk as late as it can go, knowing that even after sunset, there's a gap before the entire sky goes the shade of night.

Ryan has him pull over a couple of minutes before his house will appear.

"This is a good spot," he tells Avery. "I don't want to say goodbye in front of my house, if you know what I mean."

Avery thinks he knows what Ryan means, knows what Ryan wants to do, and immediately all of his senses are reaching out for it. The radio is on low, the dashboard glowing dimly in the increasing twilight.

"I've had a great time," Avery says, because he feels it needs to be said.

"Me too," Ryan murmurs. And it is the shift into that murmur that marks the turning within the car. Avery suddenly feels that he is breathing electric air, and it is through this air that Ryan is leaning. Avery leans into it, too, leans into all of it, and that is when their lips touch for the first time, that is the consecration of everything they've already known.

This is what we don't admit about first kisses: One of the most gratifying things about them is that they are proof, actual proof, that the other person wants to kiss us.

We are desirable. We desire.

Every kiss that matters contains a recognition at its core.

*   *   *

Cooper returns to Starbucks a few minutes before seven-thirty, just in case Antimatter—*Julian*—is early. In the interim, he's gone to Subway for dinner. And now he's finally checking his messages. Well, the first message. Which is a mistake.

"You had better get your ass back here right now if you know what's good for you. I will drag you back here myself if I have—"

Cooper hits delete. Then he hits delete thirteen more times.

We want to shake him. We want to tell him what we learned from blunt experience: While you have to listen to the first message, it's the most recent message that matters the most. Tempers can calm. Rage can wear itself out. Sense can return.

We're not saying he should go back. We know that's a hard choice. But we think he needs to hear the most recent message before he decides.

All of the messages are from his father or his mother. No one else has called. It's gotten to the point that Cooper barely notices this.

Julian is four minutes late. He looks like his photo on the app, which is a relief. Cooper is sure the person and the photo don't always match. Since he's never actually met someone from online before, he's had no experience one way or the other. He knows he looks like his own photo. It's only the words that are lies.

"Hey, there," Julian says. Cooper can't tell if he's nervous. We can tell he is.

"Hey," Cooper says back, casual. Like he does this all the time.

Julian remains standing. "Do you want to go somewhere else? Somewhere less Starbucks?"

"Like where?" Cooper asks. It comes out as a challenge.

"I don't know. I'm sorry—I should have thought about that. A drink, maybe? Oh, wait. That won't work."

"Why?"

"Um . . . your age?"

"I might be nineteen, but I'm still up for a drink."

"Do you have an ID?"

"No. But we don't have to go to a bar."

"So where . . . ?" Julian begins. Then he gets it. "I'm not sure we should go to my place. Not . . . yet."

"Why don't we stay here for a little while, then? You don't have to buy anything. I'll just get a latte, and we can talk. Okay?"

Like that, Cooper's taken charge. And he gets a charge from that.

It's enough, for now, to balance out his disappointment. Cooper figures this guy isn't a dream and he isn't a nightmare. He's just more of the same, better probably than Cooper feels he deserves. But at least there's the possibility that the night will go a little differently than it usually does.

The sun retreats from the sky, and the light around Harry and Craig darkens. The lamps above them go on, and it's a harsher light than Tariq had imagined it would be. If you look on the feed, Harry and Craig appear to be bleached-out blurs immersed in shadow.

The drama club springs to action. Most of them have stayed here after rehearsal, cheering on Harry and Craig. The head of the tech crew calls their advisor for permission, then instructs his squad to start running more extension cords from the school. Tariq is consulted, and spotlights are obtained. The tech crew works quietly. Smita expresses gratitude, and they are almost embarrassed by it. It's one of the rules of tech crew: If you are nice to them, they will help you. If you are mean to them—if you push them into lockers, if you call them names, if you make it clear you think less of them—then they will burn you the first chance they get, and they will enjoy it. Harry and Craig have always been cool to them, so they're pitching in.

Within an hour the whole place is rigged. Harry is grateful for the distraction. His feet feel like uncomfortable blocks of cement, no matter how often he moves them. He is also starting to feel his eyelids grow heavier, so he signals an *E* and gets an energy drink. It's a tricky operation—kissing Craig and sipping from a straw at the same time. But Craig makes sure Harry's covered, and gets more than a few drops of energy drink in his own mouth as a result. Almost immediately, Harry can feel his heart race as the drink goes through his system. He'll be good for a few hours, and then might need another boost. Luckily, his bladder is behaving.

Craig is upset, but not surprised, that his mother hasn't returned. That must have been his father's order. To ignore. To deny.

He could text her. He could beg her to come back. He could ask her what's going on.

But he stops himself. His parents have to figure it out them-selves. Because he's not the one with the problem—they are.

Harry senses him drifting. He pulls Craig closer. Kisses him like he means it. Kisses him to draw him back.

People cheer. But not everyone. At this point there are peo-ple in the crowd who aren't smiling at all. Their disgust would be visible to anyone next to them, if the people next to them were watching. But for now they are invisible—except to us. We see them, and we have no doubt they will not stay invisible. Not for long.

The night pushes on.

"Don't mind the mess," Julian says as he turns the key in the door.

Cooper promises he won't. He'd bet his room is messier, anyway.

Sure enough, when he gets in the apartment, he doesn't know what Julian's talking about. Everything seems to be in order. It's not that big a place, but it's not like there's underwear every-where, or pipes leaking through the ceiling. There are canvases in various states of completion all over the living room.

Julian sees Cooper looking, and feels the need to explain. "It's just the way I work—I'll spend an hour on one thing, then switch to something else, then switch again. I'm usually work-ing on at least twenty paintings at the same time. Very ADD, I know. But I've tried doing it the other way, and the paintings get tired."

Cooper gestures at the painting on the easel. "Is that your mom or something?"

Julian blushes. "No. It's actually Joni Mitchell. I listen to her a lot when I paint, so I figured I'd return the favor. Although I'm not sure she'd appreciate the gesture. Did you know she's a painter, too?"

Cooper clearly has no idea what Julian's talking about, and when Julian realizes this, he blushes further.

"I'm being a bad host," he says. "I haven't even offered you a drink yet, Drake. What do you want?"

Cooper almost trips up on that *Drake*—he's forgotten that's his name right now. But he recovers quickly, and asks for a Jack and Coke. He's never really had a drink with anyone else before, just in the company of his dad's liquor cabinet when his parents have been away. Jack and Coke is the first thing that comes to his mind.

"It might have to be a Jack and Diet Coke," Julian says. "Let me check." He goes into the kitchen and yells out, "Yeah, Diet Coke."

"That's fine!" Cooper yells back.

Cooper can hear the ice maker doing its work, then the clink of ice cubes being dropped into glasses, and the release of the Diet Coke bottle when its cap is turned. He looks at some of the paintings and likes them more than he thought he would. Julian isn't bad at all. And there's something he likes about the way all of the paintings are unfinished. It seems more real that way. People are caught between being sketches and being complete. Cooper has no idea who any of them are. But he doesn't expect to, so that's okay. There's one that looks like it could be his English teacher from eighth grade. But he's sure it probably isn't, and he barely remembers her, anyway.

Julian comes in with two glasses of the same drink. Cooper likes the taste of his—there's just the right balance, the Jack tasting like alcoholic caramel at the core of the chemical Diet Coke fizz. Julian asks him who his favorite painter is, and Cooper says Picasso, because that's the first painter he can think of. Then Julian asks him what his favorite period of Picasso's is, and from the recesses of his mind, the phrase *blue period* rises, so that's his answer, and from Julian's pleased reaction, he can tell it's a good one.

Julian goes off on a tangent about how the Impressionists are overappreciated by the general population, which leads to them being underappreciated by art snobs. Cooper polishes off his drink and wants Julian to stop talking about Monet, because it wasn't an art appreciation app they met on, it was a sex app. Julian realizes he's lost Cooper and ties off the sentence he's speaking, then takes a sip of his own quarter-empty drink. "Let me put on some music," he says, and asks if Cooper has any requests. Cooper says whatever is fine with him, then is impressed when Julian goes over to his computer and puts on some Arcade Fire.

"I like them," Cooper says, and even though it's just three words, he feels strange saying them, as if he's just given something away.

"Me too," Julian says, and takes another sip.

Cooper wants something to start, and he wants it to start now. So he moves closer to Julian. Much closer. Undeniably closer. Julian is about to begin a sentence, but Cooper's movement blocks it. Cooper thinks: *This is what we're after, isn't it?* He puts his glass down, careful not to put it too close to any of the paintings. It's time to move in. He's seen so many scenes of guys doing this—gotten hard to them doing this, jerked off to them doing this. Now here it is. Julian's got a great body, a nice face. Cooper wants to see what will happen, wants to see if this changes anything. Julian's putting down his own drink, running his hand down Cooper's arm. Cooper knows he has him, knows he has it. He reaches out and puts his hand on the side of Julian's neck. Leans in. And here it is, them pressing their mouths together, pressing their bodies together. Cooper wants it so badly, wants something, and he doesn't want to stop for breath, he wants to keep going and going. It's Julian who pulls away for a second, who actually asks if this is okay. And Cooper says yes, of course it's okay, and then they're pressing back in. It's what he thought it would be and it's not what he'd thought it would be, because Julian is gentler than he imagined a stranger would be, and when Cooper tries to push it harder, Julian slows it down. It's a subtle disagreement, and they play it like the game it is. Cooper wants to pull him down to the couch, wants to get him horizontal, but the couch is covered in paintings, so he lets it go on for a little bit longer, then surfaces and asks, "The bedroom?" And when Julian gives him a surprised look, he says, "I don't want to crush your paintings." Julian smiles at that, takes him by the hand, and they're in the tiny bedroom, still standing up and kissing, so Cooper topples them over onto the bed. Julian laughs, and Cooper kisses that laugh. It goes away, the laugh, and instead there are hands exploring—Cooper, not knowing any better, moves out of sequence, goes right for the groin, and Julian pulls away, directs him back above the waist, but Cooper's not satisfied, Cooper's not feeling what he wants to feel. He retreats for a few minutes, kissing with him on top, then rolling them over so they're kissing with him on the bottom, groins touching now, him feeling what's going on beneath Julian's jeans, then rolling over again so he can take off his shirt and then take off Julian's shirt. Now it's skin on skin, sweat on sweat, and it's hot, it's really hot, but Cooper's still not feeling what he wants to feel—it still feels empty to him—he's still feeling empty—so he kisses Julian harder, moves his hands down there, and Julian whispers, "Not yet," and Cooper feels he can't wait much longer, it's going too slow and he wants it to be fast enough that he doesn't feel anything else, doesn't think anything else, because isn't that what sex is supposed to be like, isn't it supposed to be a form of oblivion, and he's not there yet—not there—and Julian is slowing things down again, easing things down, and Cooper doesn't understand why they're not naked yet, so he moves to Julian's belt, but Julian moves them around so it's impossible to undo the buckle. Cooper goes for the buttons on his own jeans, only Julian takes his hand, forces his hands up so they're over his head, and Cooper likes the strong movement of that, likes the force, feels Julian's chest hair against his bare chest, gasps involuntarily when Julian kisses his neck, then the intersection of his neck and his shoulder blade, a spot he didn't even know he had. He wants more, even more, so he bends them so they're side by side, moves his hands down, disengages them from Julian's, starts innocently enough at his shoulders, but then thrusts them down, down, and Julian's hands are there again, blocking him.

Julian says, "Let's go a little slower. It's just the first date." And Cooper wants to tell him they're only going to have a first date, so they might as well go all the way, might as well see what's going on under those jeans. If this were porn, they'd be naked by now, they'd be blowing each other. But of course he doesn't say that, doesn't say this is the only date they're going to have, doesn't want to end things entirely, wants to deny that maybe somewhere in his mind he was hoping he would find a boyfriend tonight, because everybody knows you don't go on a sex app to find a boyfriend, and Julian would never want to be with him, anyway, because Julian thinks that right now he's tonguing the nipple of a nineteen-year-old college student with two roommates back home, a nineteen-year-old college student who has his shit together, and Cooper's thinking, *Where's the oblivion?* because now even his body is starting to fall out of it, and that's ridiculous because he's a seventeen-year-old boy and a breeze can make him hard, and while he's still hard, he feels like it's not going to go anywhere, and now Julian realizes they've fallen out of step, and he curls away, lies back on a pillow, leans on his side and strokes Cooper's shoulder, touches Cooper's cheek, says, "You're so lovely," and Cooper doesn't want to be lovely, he doesn't want to be a painting, he wants to be screwing himself into oblivion, and he knows, completely knows, that Julian is not the guy for the job. In fact, the only guy for the job would probably be someone who didn't give a shit at all about him, and that would only be worse. So this is one path ended. This is one relief crossed out. Julian asks, "Are you okay?" And Cooper says he's great, because what's one more empty lie? Julian kisses him again, and then they exist like that, half entwined, Julian touching his hair, his chest. Breathing softly, trying to wrap them inside something softer than regular life. Cooper knows he should feel lovely, or at least relaxed. But lying there, he feels like he's made of stone. Or no, not even stone. He feels like flesh. Not skin, not heartbeat. Just flesh. Julian is treating him like someone special, but Julian doesn't know anything at all, because Cooper's a piece of shit, and Julian's lying there, admiring it.

He closes his eyes, feels the touch, but not any sensation from it. Time expands, and then he opens his eyes and looks at the clock and it contracts. Cooper must have slept for a little bit. Julian must have joined him. Now Cooper startles awake, and Julian shifts beside him. "What time is it?" Julian mumbles, and then they see what time it is, which is later than either of them want it to be. "We must have drifted off," Julian says with a smile. He stands up, puts his shirt on, then warns Cooper before he turns on the light. "I think we need to call it a night," Julian tells him. "I have first shift tomorrow morning—I have to get up at five-thirty. So I should probably get to sleep. Or get back to sleep, as the case may be. Let me drive you back to your car. Or walk you back."

The thought of his car depresses him. But even so, Cooper cannot believe what he says next. Even as the words are leaving his lips, he cannot believe he is saying them. He hates himself deeply for saying them. They make him feel like he's nine.

"Could I maybe stay here tonight?" he asks.

Julian is not expecting this. He looks at Cooper's shirt, tangled on the floor.

"Not this time, okay?" he says. "I know it sounds silly, but that's a big step for me. Plus, I have to get up so damn early. Another time."

The next words that want to emerge from Cooper's mouth are *I can sleep on the couch*. But this time he manages to trap them, swallow them back down. Were he a better liar, he could probably craft a story to justify the statement (a wild party in the dorm, a roommate's boyfriend or girlfriend over, a feeling the Jack and Coke is hitting him too hard to drive). But the lies are as inaccessible to him as the truth is to Julian.

Cooper reaches down for his shirt and puts it on, then re-places the change that fell out of his pocket as he and Julian were rolling around. He tells Julian he doesn't need to drive him or walk him to his car. He says he could use the walk, and that he doesn't have nearly as early a start as Julian does. Julian hasn't put on his shoes yet, and because of this, and because Cooper doesn't really look like he wants the company, he backs down. Together they walk out of the bedroom, to the front door. Julian kisses him again, but Cooper barely feels it at this point. Before Julian opens the door, he asks Cooper for his phone number. Cooper gives him a fake.

"I hope I'll see you again," Julian says in parting.

"Yeah, thanks," Cooper replies. Then he's out the door.

For a moment when he gets outside, the air feels good. But that's only because he isn't thinking about anything else.

Then he starts to think about other things, and he doesn't feel good. The noise has come to claim him again. The flat, dead noise.

* * *

We watch as Julian takes the two glasses into the kitchen, the ice cubes melted now. We watch as he puts them in the sink, then stands over the sink, both hands on the counter, wondering what just happened.

Miles away, Peter and Neil are feeling much more certainty. After dinner, they hid in the basement and made out for a while—an intense interlude that came to a mutually pleasing conclusion. Then they went online and chatted with friends, many of whom were also watching the Big Kiss. Finally, it was time for Neil to head home, so now they are saying their usual goodnights: Peter in his boxers, Neil in his pajamas.

"I could kiss you for hours and still be on my feet," Peter says.

"Likewise," Neil says.

Then they wave, and sign off into slumber.

Ryan texts Avery to say goodnight, and asks him what he's doing tomorrow. Would he be up for another drive?

Avery has about a million other things to do, but of course he says he's free. Completely free.

He should be floating from the day, but a look in the mirror drags him down. He has a full-length mirror in his bedroom, and it is often his enemy. Tonight he looks into it and tries to see what Ryan sees, and all he gets in return is disappointment. He's worked so hard to change his body, to make it the right body, but he can't come close to loving it. He thinks it's because he was born in the wrong body, but we want to whisper in his ears that many of us were born in the right bodies and *still* felt foreign inside them, felt betrayed. We completely misunderstood our bodies. We punished them, berated them, held them to an Olympian ideal that was deeply unfair to them. We loathed the hair in some places and the lack of hair in others. We wanted everything to be tighter, stronger, harder, faster. We rarely recognized our own beauty unless someone else was recognizing it for us. We starved or we pushed or we hid or we paraded, and there was always another body we thought was better than ours. There was always something wrong, most of the time numerous things wrong. When we were healthy, we were ignorant. We could never be content within our own skin.

Breathe, we want to tell Avery. *Feel yourself breathe. Because that is as much a part of your body as anything else.*

Avery, we whisper, *you are a marvel.*

And he is. He may never believe it, but he is.

It's eleven o'clock on a Saturday night. Since there is rarely anything to do on a Saturday night in Harry and Craig's town, a lot of people are dropping by the lawn of the high school to see the two boys kissing. A multitude of cell phone pictures is being taken—the disposable commemoration of this day and age. Sometimes girls have to shush their drunken boyfriends, who want to say something inappropriate. Or maybe the boyfriends say it quietly, and the girlfriends laugh. Not everybody is here to show support. Some are just here because they think it's a freak show.

"I bet if we wanted to break the world record with a *straight* kiss, they'd never give us the high school," one guy complains, as if this is a particular aspiration that's been robbed from him.

"Totally," his girlfriend agrees.

"This is bullshit," another guy loudly declares, his voice and confidence amplified by the Budweiser he's consumed.

You're bullshit, the drama club girl next to him wants to say.

Eventually the crowd thins out—there's not much to see after a while. It's getting late, a little chilly. People get back into their cars—some to go to late-night parties, but most to go home.

Even within Harry and Craig's team—that's what they think of themselves now, over eleven hours into it—there's a shift change. Harry's mom blows a kiss to both Harry and Craig, then goes home to get some rest. She'll see them in the morning. Rachel also heads home, so she can relieve Tariq later on, even though he's pledged to stay up the whole time. Smita promised her mother she'd be home by one. Mykal has a schedule of a few friends who are sleeping now but who will come in the middle of the night, bearing glow sticks and caffeine.

It's also the end of Mr. Nichol's shift. As his replacement comes closer, we can't believe our eyes.

Look, look, we tell each other. *It's Tom!*

He's Mr. Bellamy to his history students. But he's Tom to us. Tom! It's so good to see him. So wonderful to see him. Tom is one of us. Tom went through it all with us. Tom made it through. He was there in the hospital with so many of us, the archangel of St. Vincent's, our healthier version, prodding the doctors and calling over the nurses and holding our hands and holding the hands of our partners, our parents, our little sisters—anyone who had a hand to be held. He had to watch so many of us die, had to say goodbye so many times. Outside of our rooms he would get angry, upset, despairing. But when he was with us, it was like he was powered solely by an engine of grace. Even the people who loved us would hesitate at first to touch us—more from the shock of our diminishment, from the strangeness of how we were both gone and present, not who we were but still who we were. Tom became used to this. First because of Dennis, the way he stayed with Dennis until the very end. He could have left after that, after Dennis was gone. We wouldn't have blamed him. But he stayed. When his friends got sick, he was there. And for those of us he'd never known before—he was always a smile in the room, always a touch on the shoulder, a light flirtation that we needed. They should have made him a nurse. They should have made him mayor. He lost years of his life to us, although that's not the story he'd tell. He would say he gained. And he'd say he was lucky, because when he came down with it, when his blood turned against him, it was a little later on and the cocktail was starting to work. So he lived. He made it to a different kind of after from the rest of us. It is still an after. Every day it feels to him like an after. But he is here. He is living.

A history teacher. An out, outspoken history teacher. The kind of history teacher we never would have had. But this is what losing most of your friends does: It makes you unafraid. Whatever anyone threatens, whatever anyone is offended by, it doesn't matter, because you have already survived much, much worse. In fact, you are still surviving. You survive every single, blessed day.

It makes sense for Tom to be here. It wouldn't be the same without him.

And it makes sense for him to have taken the hardest shift. The night watch.

Mr. Nichol passes him the stopwatch. Tom walks over and says hello to Harry and Craig. He's been watching the feed, but it's even more powerful to see these boys in person. He gestures to them, like a rabbi or a priest offering a benediction.

"Keep going," he says. "You're doing great."

Mrs. Archer, Harry's next-door neighbor, has brought over coffee, and offers Tom a cup. He takes it gratefully.

He wants to be wide awake for all of this.

Every now and then he looks to the sky.

We reach midnight. Tariq can't keep up with all the comments. Even with Harry and Craig on their phones, also answering, there are too many people to thank one by one. Tariq had thought it would slow down as it got late, as people started to go to bed. But he hadn't been counting on it becoming so global. As people go to sleep in New Jersey, they are waking up in Germany. Australia's heading into the afternoon. Tokyo, too. Because of the pink-haired blogger and all the other posts that have echoed out, word is passed on and passed on and passed on. Rachel hastily put together a Facebook page, and it already has fifty thousand fans.

Tariq is exchanging chat messages with someone from the site that's hosting the feed, making sure there's enough bandwidth, when he hears an engine gunning behind him, like a truck passing by.

There's a shout:

"FAAAAAAAAAGGOTS! DIRTY FAAAAAGGOTS!"

Then laughter and cheers coming from the car that's making the noise. Everyone turns, and the car rolls through the parking lot, turns around for another pass.

"YOU'RE NOTHING BUT FAAAAAGGOTS!"

Because of the spotlights, it's hard to see outside of their circle, hard to see anything besides headlights and a blurry head leaning out the passenger window. Tariq feels himself freezing. He knows these guys aren't going to get out of the car, aren't going to come over here with all the cameras going and the police officer and so many witnesses. But still, his instinct is fear.

Harry and Craig hear it too. Craig flinches at the sound, and Harry is a mix of amused and pissed. He refuses to take drunk shitheads seriously. He watches as the police officer half-heartedly takes a few steps away from the taped-off area, tries to get a better view of the car. But it's already speeding away, point made. Harry's father is asking Tariq and Smita if they know who it was, if it was kids from the high school. But neither of them know. Mykal asks around.

Harry gestures an M for music, then indicates that Tariq should turn it up. Tariq's planned his playlist well—there's not a ballad within earshot at this time of the night. Instead it's all Lady Gaga, Pink, Kylie, Madonna, Whitney, Beyoncé— the gay Sirens, here to lure you away from sleep and onto the dance floor. Tariq's found an "Express Yourself/Born This Way" mash-up, and as he turns it up, Harry convinces Craig to dance with him. If they're going to be faggots, they're going to be dancing faggots. Dancing, *kissing* faggots.

Tariq's pulse is still racing, but he lets the music take off the edge, take him away from what just happened. He starts to sway along, show some moves, imagine this is their club, their space, their domain. Smita gets into the groove, too, and even Mr. Bellamy starts to dance in a grown-up kind of way. Tariq can't believe it when Mr. Ramirez and Mrs. Archer, the coffee-bringing neighbor, start to sing along. They probably know the songs from *Glee*—who knows? The police officer now on shift is the only one not joining in, but Tariq is pretty sure there's some Zeppelin later in the mix for him.

It's crazy, because Harry is feeling fully conscious again. Is he completely tired of kissing Craig? Oh, totally. They've both been tired of it for hours at this point. But that's the challenge, to get through all that. If you're running a marathon, you're not expecting to find pleasure in every step. The music is helping, reminding him that the time after midnight can be used for things other than sleeping.

He feels something hit his back, and at first he doesn't understand what it is. It could almost be Craig's hand, marking the beat. But then the second egg hits him right on the side of his head. He hears it breaking beside his ear. Feels the shock of it, the slime of it. Another hits his leg. His instinct is to recoil, to turn. But luckily Craig is there, right there, to reach his hand up to shield him, to reach up his hand to remind Harry to stay where he is. The yolk is beginning to run down his face, down his neck. Craig tries to wipe it away, as Harry's father shouts something, goes running into the darkness beyond the lights. The police officer is on alert now, talking into his radio. Smita is hurrying over with a towel so Craig can get the egg off Harry's face. (No one else is allowed to touch them, lest it be construed as "propping.") Tariq is stopped cold for a second, looking in the direction Mr. Ramirez went, wondering what he should do. He looks at his computer, and the feed comments are going crazy, everyone asking, *What was that? What's happening?* So now he has something to do, and stupidly he finds himself calling out to Harry and Craig, "Keep kissing!" Because that's what he needs to see right now, that's what everyone needs to see. But Harry is shaking. He can't help it—he's shaking. He can't believe what happened, and knows he shouldn't be embarrassed, but he is. He feels reduced, ridiculed. By shitheads. He can smell the egg, smell it on his skin. Even though Smita's dampening the towel with bottled water now so Craig can get it all off, he can still feel it on his skin, the shock of its impact.

His father comes back empty-handed, says something to the police officer. No way to tell who it was. They ran away on foot. Could have gone in any direction. Mr. Ramirez thinks it was more than one kid. But it was hard to tell in the dark.

Craig feels Harry shivering. He holds Harry closer, feels the egg stain on the back of Harry's shirt. Craig makes a C sign with his hand—*clothes*—and points to Harry. Mr. Bellamy understands and offers Harry a hoodie. Harry is shivering harder now, and Craig has to hold the back of his head, to make sure he doesn't shiver away from him. Harry holds out his arms so Craig can help him put on the hoodie, one arm at a time. It feels strange to be dressed in this way, but he's grateful for the warmth.

It's over, he tells himself.

But it's not over. Not yet. Because now there are voices in the dark. Voices getting closer. And pinpoints of light—flashlights. It is 12:23 in the morning, and people are coming to be here, coming to help. They saw what happened, and they can't stay in their houses. Not just Harry and Craig's friends. But their friends' parents, too. Jim from the tech crew has sped over with more lights from his basement. There have to be at least a dozen people. Then more than a dozen. Smita's mom is here. Two more police officers. And a man Harry's never seen before walks up and goes straight to Mr. Bellamy, saying, "I'm staying right here with you." They wear matching rings.

The site becomes a hive of activity. Jim puts up more lights so the lawn can be seen more clearly. And whereas before when people watched, they did so in conversational clumps, now they make a line, a wall, between Harry and Craig and the outside world. Protecting them.

The whole time, the music hasn't stopped. "Can't Get You Out of My Head" is pumping through the air. Harry senses Craig coming alert to something. He looks off to the side and sees the two figures coming closer.

Craig's mother. His oldest brother, Sam, a senior at the high school.

They head right to Craig, and Craig's mother asks him if he's okay.

He nods slightly.

"Sam was watching, and he came to get us."

Us. Craig hears the *us*, and at first doesn't understand it. Then his father and his other brother, Kevin, are there, too.

"Parked the car," Craig's father says. "Your mom couldn't wait."

It hits Craig fully: He is, right now, *kissing Harry right in front of his father*. His mind can't really acclimate to this. At all.

Harry's dad comes over to introduce himself to Craig's father and brothers, and also, more subtly, to make sure they don't end up blocking all of the cameras. Craig can see his father measure Harry's dad up; for his part, Harry's dad is trying his hardest to make a good impression.

Kevin, a seventh grader, seems to not understand why he was woken up for this. Sam, though, keeps staring at Craig. Ten minutes ago, if you'd told Craig that Sam had been in the car with the guys yelling "FAGGOTS!", he wouldn't have been that surprised. But now he has to accept that his brother's staring is more complicated than that. It's not an older-brother death stare. He's probably just trying to understand the situation as much as Craig is.

"We're not staying for long," Craig's father is saying.

"But we just got here," Kevin whines.

"It's late. We wanted to make sure he's okay, and he's okay."

Craig can feel his father keeping his distance—but still, he's closer than Craig thought he would be. He wonders what his mother said to him, how she explained.

"I'm going to stay," Sam mumbles.

Craig's father does not look happy with this.

"It's well after midnight," he intones. "You're coming home."

Sam smiles mischievously and says, "But *Craig* gets to stay out. . . ."

Craig can feel the tremor of Harry's laugh at this line.

Craig's father doesn't think it's funny, though.

"Don't push me," he says. "This is about as far as I can go."

Craig can see Sam considering it. He tries to use his eyes to implore his brother, *Just go*. Not that Sam has ever listened to him before.

Craig's mom steps in. "We can all come back tomorrow," she says, shepherding Sam back in the direction of the car.

"We'll be here!" Harry's dad says, maybe a little too cheerily.

Craig's mom takes in the wall of supporters that has formed. When she turns back to Craig, it's hard to read the expression on her face. Or maybe that's what's being expressed: a complete lack of definition.

Craig points toward the parking lot, then makes an okay sign. So she knows it's okay for her to go. Even though nobody's asked him.

Just as quickly as they appeared, his family heads back home.

The two of them have twenty-three hours to go.

Harry can still smell the egg on his skin.

At two in the morning, Cooper wakes up in the backseat of his own car. His body is sore from trying to fit. The seat belt has been digging into his back. He looks at his watch and feels only disappointment in the hour—he wants it to be five or six or oblivion. He has never slept in his car before, and he doesn't know how long he'll be able to do it. If this is his life now, if this is what his life has become, it's even more pathetic to him than it was before. He should have taken clothes with him. He should have taken food. There aren't even voices in his head telling him this—it would be much easier if there were voices, because then it could be a conversation. But these are things that he *knows*, and no voice needs to bother to say them. He could try to distract himself with his phone, but the battery's low and the car needs to be on to work the charger. He's sick of the phone, too. Sick of the men and the boys. Sick of everyone wanting so badly to be turned on that they become these one-track minds living from one one-track minute to the next. And where does that track lead? Men and boys all across America getting off, and not a single one cares about Cooper. Yeah, if they read about him in the paper, they'd be sad. But Cooper doesn't think they'd realize it was him, the boy they were chatting with last night.

Cooper doesn't believe tomorrow will be better. Or any tomorrow. Not really. We want to tell him in a thousand different ways that he's wrong. But who are we? Even if we could speak, even if we could knock on that window and get him to roll it down, he would never believe what we have to say, not compared to what he believes about himself, and about the world.

His mind is on fire now, and it will be hours until it cools itself back into the right temperature for sleep. He is angry at his father, angry at his mother, but mostly he's come to feel that all this was inevitable, that he was born to be a boy who must sleep in his car, that there was no way he was going to make it through high school without being caught. He feels he's been soured by his own desires, squandered by his own impulses. He despises himself, and that is the flame that sets his mind on fire.

He is too tired to do anything about it. Too tired to turn on the car to charge his phone. Too tired to figure out a better place to be. Too tired to run away somewhere. Too tired to end it all. So he stays in that back seat, contorting himself but never finding comfort. Unable to sleep. Unable to live. Unable to leave.

We would wake in the middle of the night. Sometimes there were tubes down our throats. Sometimes we were attached to machines that seemed more alive than we were. Sometimes the darkness was laced with light. Sometimes we had been dreaming we were home, and that our mother was in the next room. We didn't know the room we woke into, or we knew it too well. The last stop. Final destination. And there we were, trapped in those endless, unforgiving hours. Unable to sleep. Unable to live. Unable to leave.

The world is quieter now. It is never quiet, but it can get quieter. What strange creatures we are, to find silence peaceful, when permanent silence is the thing we most dread. Nighttime is not that. Nighttime still rustles, still creaks and whispers and trembles in its throat. It is not darkness we fear, but our own helplessness within it. How merciful to have been granted the other senses.

There are very few lights on in this town at four in the morning. Most of the ones that are on were left on by accident.

There are one or two night readers, one or two night wanderers, one or two night workers to be found. But most everyone else is asleep.

We are the ones who are awake.

Except on the front lawn of the local high school. There, two boys remain kissing. Muscles sore, mouths tired, eyelids weighty, Harry and Craig hold on to each other, hold on to the forces inside them that will keep them awake. At four in the morning, you can be so light-headed that even the stars seem to have a sound. Harry and Craig sway to the sound of those stars—the few that glimmer over their heads—but also to the sound of all of the unseen stars, all the nebulae that are out of reach but still present. At four in the morning, you can imagine the whole universe is looking down at you. Harry and Craig dance for the universe, and also for the friends who have gathered, the ring of people that remains around them. Mr. Ramirez is snoring lightly in his chair. Tariq's fingers tap out a language on his keyboard as he responds to questions from Rome and Edinburgh and Dubai. Smita's mom takes orders for coffee. Jim laughs at something another boy from tech crew has said. Mr. Bellamy, our Tom, tells his husband all is well, that he should go home and get some sleep. Harry and Craig dance to these sounds, too. Craig needs to be held, and Harry is holding him. Harry is letting his mind wander—to books he's read, to movies he's seen, to things he may want to say to the tens of thousands of people who are watching them. But Craig's mind doesn't wander much farther than Harry. With everything that's happened, Craig is retreating into the closeness of Harry, the familiarity of his body, of him. This is what he missed when it was gone, what his loneliness calls out for. He knows the reason Harry is kissing him, but he still feels it as a kiss. He can't help it, because it helps him. He can't help it, because right now he needs it so much.

He is not wrong to do this. When you need to hold on to something, you should. Whatever gets you through, take it.

Harry needs him, too. Even if he's not concentrating on that need right now, it's there. He is so safe within it that he hardly realizes it's present. Like the coolness of the night, like the small sounds that soundtrack the stars.

We know what it's like to need to hold on. We hold on to you. Which is to say, we hold on to life.

You have music at your fingertips. Any song you want to hear, there it is.

We marvel at that. The infinite jukebox.

If we want to hear a song, we must steal the sound waves that you send into the air. But there are moments that are so palpable, so in sync with a song we once knew, that it plays itself from some long-lost cassette player that even our memory doesn't seem to control.

Like the moment Ryan wakes up and thinks of Avery, and the moment (forty minutes later) that Avery wakes up and thinks of Ryan. There is only the sound of their breathing as they blink themselves into the day, only the shift in the mattress, the accidental fall of a pillow to the floor. This should be all that we hear, but there is also the unmistakable sound of Aretha Franklin in our ears, singing "What a Diff'rence a Day Made." They both wake into happiness instead of uncertainty, into a better version of the world because yesterday was so welcome. There is no way they would articulate it in the same way Aretha does, when she bursts out with *"It's heaven, heaven, heaven when you / When you find love and romance on the menu."* Go and listen to it right now—you have it right at your fingertips, for less than the price of a candy bar. The lyrics sound old, but the music is eternal—that joy in discovering that the right person at the right time can open all the windows and unlock all the doors.

The world wakes up around Harry and Craig.

Harry lifts his feet, wiggles his toes, and only feels soreness, bloat. His back feels like sandpaper has been put between each vertebra. His neck is a wire hanger that an elephant is pulling on. His eyes are dry, but his body is damp. He still smells the egg, feels the egg. But maybe that's just what sweat smells and feels like after twenty hours. Despite the fact that he's surrounded by electricity, he finds himself wanting it to rain.

Craig wants to brush his teeth. He and Harry experimented with mouthwash when they were practicing, but it never worked—it was impossible to spit and kiss at the same time. Usually Craig's fantasies of Harry are elaborate—dancing in tuxedos across the floor of Grand Central Terminal, or canoeing on a lake as the world around them turns instantaneously from summer to fall, all the trees burning into color at once. But now the deepest, clearest fantasy Craig has is of the two of them sitting down. That's it. Him and Harry, in those two chairs right over there. Sitting down. Not even holding hands. Not kissing. Just sitting there, resting. No one else in the whole world. Just the two of them, sitting down.

We think of ourselves as creatures marked by a particular intelligence. But one of our finest features is the inability of our expectation to truly simulate the experience we are expecting. Our anticipation of joy is never the same as joy. Our anticipation of pain is never the same as pain. Our anticipation of challenge is in no way the same experience as the challenge itself. If we could feel the things we fear ahead of time, we would be traumatized. So instead we venture out thinking we know how things will feel, but knowing nothing of how things will really feel. Already, Craig and Harry are far beyond any expectation, any preparation. They must make up each minute as it comes along, and in doing so, they are creative. Yes, creative. You do not need to be writing or painting or sculpting in order to be creative. You must simply create. And this is what Craig and Harry are doing. They are creating a kiss, and they are also creating their stories, and by creating their stories, they are creating their lives.

This can be a very painful process.

We, who can no longer create, can stand for hours and days and months without feeling anything. You wouldn't think that we would miss physical pain, considering all the pain that we went through. But we do. We miss it. We miss the price we paid for life. Because it was part of life.

Craig and Harry are exhausted, to a degree we can understand well. Some might think them foolish, to put themselves through this, especially if they fail. But we understand the need to push beyond expectation, beyond preparation. We understand the desire to create, to step on new ground. To feel every ounce of space you are taking up in the world. To endure.

Around the world, screens light up. Around the world, words are flown through wires. Around the world, images are reduced to particles and, moments later, are perfectly reassembled. Around the world, people see these two boys kissing and find something there.

Around town, boys and girls wake up. Around town, men and women mobilize. Around town, complaints are made and disbelief feeds within an echo chamber. Around town, breakfast is served and breakfast is taken. Around town, it feels like an ordinary day, but also not, if you know what's happening on the lawn outside the high school.

Camera crews from local TV stations begin to arrive.

* * *

Shortly after waking, Peter is at his computer. This is what you do now to give your day topography—scan the boxes, read the news, see the chain of your friends reporting about themselves, take the 140-character expository bursts and sift through for the information you need. It's a highly deceptive world, one that constantly asks you to comment but doesn't really care what you have to say. The illusion of participation can sometimes lead to participation. But more often than not, it only leads to more illusion, dressed in the guise of reality.

The headlines on Yahoo don't require much of Peter's head. The latest exploits of a rich girl with her own TV show, the latest poll showing that for the first time ever, Americans prefer dark chocolate to milk chocolate. Peter has to take in these words before disregarding them—so much information pushing its way into your consciousness, trying to take residence so you will watch the new show, buy the new chocolate. He quickly clicks on to the feed of the two boys kissing, and is relieved to find they are still there, still kissing. Twenty-two hours gone, less than ten hours to go. He scrolls through the comments and finds a lot of encouragement and more than a few haters. These words are now in his bedroom, now in his life. How can he not take them personally? If you let the world in, you open yourself up to the world. Even if the world doesn't know that you're there.

The camera crews unload their equipment. The reporters check their makeup, gauge the light. Harry takes some satisfaction from it—attention was the point of this, and now it has come calling. Craig feels a slight uneasiness, and also a little relief that he doesn't have to worry anymore about his parents seeing this without warning, turning on the channel and finding something unexpected.

The news teams—there are three of them—are pushy. They want to ask questions, want to get close. The police officers keep them back on the other side of the non-caution tape. But still . . . they suck all the air from the area. They are the new center of gravity for the crowd. There are people now who haven't been seen before, who haven't spoken up before. There are Craig and Harry's friends, yes, but there are also people who think this is criminal, that it should be stopped, that it is an affront to the high school, to the town, to society. The cameras search them out, and they gladly allow themselves to be found.

You are always so willing to broadcast yourself. You have grown used to the ubiquity of lenses, the everpresence of cameras, whether they are in your friends' pockets or watching you from atop streetlamps. For us, it was a choice to be on camera. There was a long and labored process to retrieve an image, to draw it from film and expose it onto paper. If we broadcast ourselves, it was usually just to the other people in the room. We were all actors, just as you are all actors now. But our audience wasn't as large as yours. And our performances, like those on a stage, were fleeting, uncaptured.

Harry and Craig felt nothing when it was only their own

cameras that were on. Even as tens of thousands of people were watching, they didn't really feel the eyes on them, no more so than usual. There was the perception that the people watching were friends, not strangers. But it is different when a camera crew takes aim. It is different when they can hear the reporters telling their story from a reportorial remove. They had been thinking of themselves as a cause, but now they feel reduced to a curiosity. And they can't speak for themselves. They can't say a word. They must continue kissing.

Tariq is too shy to speak for them. In the back of his mind, he can imagine all the violent homophobes writing his name down, remembering him for later. It is Harry's father who steps up and explains their aims. It is Smita who prepares the sound bites of support. It is Mr. Bellamy—Tom—who may be risking his job to say that he is a teacher at this school and that he supports the boys one hundred percent. He doesn't identify himself as gay, but he doesn't try to hide it, either.

Craig tries to stay focused on the kissing. When distractions are manifold, it's best to remember what you are supposed to be doing.

Word travels fast, our parents would warn us. It's amusing to think of that now. We thought words had so much speed back then, but we had no idea.

Avery is driving to Kindling again. Ryan offered to drive to Marigold, then admitted he'd have to borrow someone's car to do it, since he doesn't have one of his own. Avery doesn't mind—he likes driving, likes the feel of being on the road.

At a certain spot, the music he's been listening to loops around, and he doesn't want to listen to it again. When he ejects the CD, the radio comes on—a station that's Top 40 during the afternoon and evening, but talks too much in the morning. Avery would usually just put in more music, but his ear is drawn to the word *gays* and the way it's being said. Dismissively. Contemptuously.

"This is what the gays do—they stop at nothing to be in our faces with their disgusting habits and then act like they're the ones being treated badly. I don't want to look at that, and I don't want my kids to have to look at that."

The host comes on. *"So you don't think they have the right to be there?"*

"I don't think the founders of our country really had two homosexuals on their minds when they wrote the Constitution. That's all I'm saying."

"And we have our next caller."

"I don't understand why they're not being arrested. Why aren't the police arresting them? It's a public place."

"You know the police are protecting the two boys—"

"Well, they should be ashamed of themselves and start doing their job."

"I'm with you there. Next caller."

"I think what the boys are doing is brave."

"Brave? Tell them to join the army if they want to be brave."

"To be in public—"

"They should just get a room! Next caller!"

Avery doesn't know what these people are talking about, and since he's driving, he can't go online to check. The sensation he has is a strange, difficult one. He knows these people aren't talking about him. But at the same time they *are* talking about him, in their blanket dismissal. And they're also talking about us. Because so many of them are our age or older, stuck in previous decades of thought. The gays of today, the gays of yesterday—we're all the same bother, all the same wrong. Not people, really. Just something to yell about.

"If we let this go on, what's next? Men having sex with dogs in a church? Is that free speech?"

The phrase *rush to judgment* is a silly one. When it comes to judgment, most of us don't have to rush. We don't have to even leave the couch. Our judgment is so easy to reach for.

None of these people who are talking know Craig or Harry, or even care about who Craig or Harry are. The minute you stop talking about individuals and start talking about a group, your judgment has a flaw in it. We made this mistake often enough.

"You can't have a world record if you're two guys. That's not a world record."

Avery knows he should put on the music, blot out these voices. But none of us can stop listening. Because what is more transfixing than the sound of people hating you?

In the darkest part of our hearts, we used to think that maybe they were right.

We don't think that anymore.

Cooper is driving, too, but the radio is off. He was woken by a hard pounding on his windshield—someone telling him he needed to clear out of the parking lot.

Cooper's mind is slowly working up to something. The

chemicals are gathering, some of them in the wrong places. He should be thinking about clothes, about a shower, about getting home. He should be realizing that his parents are probably going to church this morning, giving him an opportunity to sneak in and get more things. He should be figuring out a next step. He should care.

But Cooper feels at too much of a distance to truly care. It's like he's sitting in an empty movie theater, looking at a blank screen. His parents aren't going to change. The world isn't going to change. He isn't going to change. So why try? He's too tired to fight it, too tired to sneak into his own house, too tired to call some hotline or ask some contact to pretend to be his friend for an hour or two.

We know: An almost certain way to die is to believe you are already dead. Some of us never stopped fighting, never gave up. But others of us did. Others of us felt the pain had become too much, and that there was nothing left to life but the struggle for life, which was not enough reason to stay. So we signed out. We caved. But our reasons are not anything Cooper knows. If he could step out of his life for a moment, if he could see it as we see it, he would know that even though he feels it's as good as over, there are still thousands of ways it could go.

His parents call again, before they leave for church.

He turns off the phone. But he can't bring himself to throw it away.

"I hope they're giving each other AIDS," the caller tells the radio host. *"I hope that when they're dying of AIDS, they show that on*

the Internet, too, so children will know what happens if you kiss like that."

The host chuckles, asks for the next caller.

"Turn that off."

Neil has come into the kitchen, and he can't believe what his parents are listening to, with his sister right there.

"What?" his father asks, blinking up from the Sunday paper.

Neil goes over and turns off the radio. "How can you listen to that? How?"

"We weren't really listening," his mother says. "It was just on."

"The woman said she wants people to die of AIDS," Miranda, age eleven, reports.

Neil's father gives her a shushing glance. Neil's mother sighs.

"We weren't really listening," she repeats.

Neil knows he should let it go. This household operates through a series of unspoken truces, negotiated by instinct more than by actual conversation. Neil has always considered his gayness to be an open secret with his parents. They've met Peter, they know what the story is, but the story is never said out loud. Neil can lead his version of his life, and his parents can believe in their version of their good son.

But *open secret* is a lie we like to tell ourselves. It's a lie we often told ourselves, in both sickness and in health. It doesn't work, because if you feel you still have a secret, there is no way to be truly open. In the interest of self-preservation, it is sometimes best to keep something back, to keep something hidden. But there usually comes a moment—and Neil is hitting his now—when you don't want self-preservation to define who you are, or who your family is. Truces may stop the battles, but part of you will always feel like you're at war.

Neil should let it go, but he doesn't. He thinks of Craig and Harry kissing, even though he can't remember their names. He thinks of Peter, and of how Peter's parents take Neil in, extend their family so that he's like a member. He thinks of his sister listening to the trash talk on the radio and his parents letting it go unanswered.

"How can you not hear that?" he asks his mother. "When something like that is being said, how can you just sit there?"

Neil never talks to his mother like this. Not since he was little, not since it was forced out of him by punishment after punishment.

His father steps in, conciliatory. He is always the good cop. Neil is tired of his parents being cops at all.

"We really didn't hear it. If we had, we would have turned it off. We were listening to the news at the top of the hour and left it on."

"When someone talks like that, you *should* hear it!" Neil says, his voice rising.

His mother looks at him like he's an incompetent employee. "Why should we hear it?"

"Because you have a gay son."

Miranda's jaw drops theatrically. This is, to her, the most interesting family conversation to ever, ever happen. Neil couldn't have shocked them more if he'd used a dirty word.

131

He's broken the truce.

"Neil . . . ," his dad begins, his tone half warning, half sympathy.

"No. If some asshole on the radio was saying that all immigrants should go back to the countries they're from, you'd pay attention. Even if you weren't listening, you'd hear it. If they were saying they hope that all Koreans die of AIDS, your blood would boil higher with every single word. But when it's gays they're talking about, you let it slide. You don't bother to hear it. It's *acceptable* to you. Even if you don't agree with it—and I am not saying you want me to get AIDS from kissing Peter—you accept it when someone else says it. You *let it happen*."

We tried to tell them what was happening. We tried to tell them the disease was spreading. We needed doctors. We needed scientists. Most of all, we needed money, and to get money, we needed attention. We put our lives in other people's hands, and for the most part, they looked at us blankly and said, *What lives? What hands?*

"I am gay. I have always been gay. I will always be gay. You have to understand that, and you have to understand that we are not really a family until you understand that."

Neil's father shakes his head. "Of course we're a family! How can you say we're not a family?"

"What has gotten into you?" his mother asks. "Your sister is right here. This isn't appropriate conversation for your sister."

Appropriate. The word is a well-dressed cage, used to capture the truth and hang it in a room that no one ventures into.

"She needs to hear this," Neil says. "Why shouldn't she hear this? You know I'm gay, don't you, Miranda?"

"Totally," Miranda answers.

"So there are no big revelations here. You all know I'm gay. You all know I have a boyfriend."

But he's never used that word before. It's always been *I'm going over to Peter's house*. Or *I'm going to the movies with Peter*. His mother once saw them holding hands as they watched a movie. That's the only reason he's sure they know.

"Yes, Neil," Mrs. Kim says, not bothering to hide the irritation in her voice. She picks the paper back up. "Now if we can get back to our Sunday morning . . ."

Neil feels he should be pleased by this brief acknowledgment, should take the truce that's being offered once more. The conversation is clearly at its end. His mother has started reading the paper again, and his father is telling him to have some breakfast. We figure this is it, this is all—most of us found acceptance through small steps such as these. Our families were rarely willing to make leaps, at least not until the end.

But it's not enough for Neil. He feels if he accepts the truce now, it will be months, maybe years, before he gets to this point again.

"I need you to say it," he tells them. "I need to hear you say it."

Mrs. Kim throws down the paper and hits the table. "What? That we're sorry? For not turning off the radio when some idiot said something idiotic? You're acting like a baby."

"No." Neil tries to keep control of his voice. "I don't need you to say you're sorry. I need you to say that I'm gay."

Neil's mother grunts and looks at his father. *You deal with this.*

"Neil," he says, "is everything okay? Why are you acting this way?"

"Just say it. Please. Just say it."

It's Miranda who speaks up. "You're gay," she says, with complete seriousness. "And I love you."

Tears spring to Neil's eyes. "Thank you, Miranda," he says. Then he looks to his parents.

"Neil . . . ," his father says.

"Please."

"Why is this so important to you?" his mother asks. "Why are you doing this?"

"I just want you to say it. That's all."

"I don't have to tell you that you have black hair, do I? I don't have to tell you that you're a boy. Why should I have to tell you this? We know, Neil. Is that what you want to hear? We know."

"But you don't mind about the other things—that I have dark hair, that I'm a boy. You mind that I'm gay. Which is why I need you to say it."

"Just say it," Miranda chimes in.

Just say it, we implore.

Miranda's words make their mother angrier. "Do you see what you're doing to your sister?" She picks up the paper and pushes back her chair.

Please.

When Neil's mother caught him and Peter holding hands, he was relieved. Relieved that it was undeniable proof. Relieved that he hadn't had to say a word.

But then she didn't say a word. If Peter hadn't been in the room, he would have thought he'd made the whole thing up.

"You're gay," his father says now.

"And Peter is my boyfriend," he says.

"And Peter is your boyfriend."

Miranda reaches out and holds her father's hand. They all look to Mrs. Kim. We all look to Mrs. Kim.

"Why does this mean so much to you?" she asks.

"Because you're my mother."

So many of us had to make our own families. So many of us had to pretend when we were home. So many of us had to leave. But every single one of us wishes we hadn't had to. Every single one of us wishes our family had acted like our family, that even when we found a new family, we hadn't had to leave the other one behind. Every single one of us would have loved to have been loved unconditionally by our parents.

Don't make him leave you, we want to tell Mrs. Kim. *He doesn't want to leave you.*

She genuinely doesn't understand what it means to hear the words out loud. She genuinely doesn't fathom why it's such a big deal for Neil to hear his parents say that he's gay, to say it like a fact, to grant it the articulation of her voice.

Mrs. Kim stands there, newspaper in her hand. She stands there and looks at her son. Both mother and son are coiled and lost in their own defensiveness. There is something plaintive in Neil's argument, a vulnerability that can easily be overlooked in the heat of battle. He wants a truce, desperately wants a truce, but this time he wants a truce on his terms, not theirs. Mrs. Kim recognizes this. Even if the memory doesn't actually play for her, she feels the echoes of the moment she told her mother she was going to start a new life, thousands of miles away. That her mind was made up and there was nothing her mother could do to stop her. How much had she wanted her mother to say,

I understand? How much had she wanted her mother to be on her side?

In fairy tales, the mother often needs to be dead. In mythology, the father must die for a prince to become a king.

But who wants a family life like fairy tales, like mythology?

You're gay. Mrs. Kim can hear the words in her head. She can hear them clearly. Once she's said them to herself, it should be easy to say them out loud. But still she hesitates, for the same reason that Neil needs so much to hear it.

Saying the truth out loud makes it more real.

Peter is your boyfriend.

Somehow, this seems a safer place to start. So she looks at her son and says it.

"Peter is your boyfriend."

That would be enough for Neil. Just to hear these words from his mother. Because the implications are clear, even if not said.

But it's not enough for Miranda.

"*And,*" she says.

The strangest thing happens then. Mrs. Kim smiles. Her daughter's irritation has made her smile, and has given her the springboard she needs to take the dive.

"*And,*" she says, "Neil is gay." She looks at all three of them in turn. "Now, if that's settled, I am going to go finish my paper in the den."

There will be no embraces here. No tears besides Neil's. No further conversation. Unless you count Mr. Kim telling his son again to have some breakfast. Unless you count Miranda's smile as he sits down, the distinct pride she feels in both him and

136

herself. Unless you count the way the words sink into Neil, the way his life feels a little more solid than it did five minutes before, the way he no longer feels the overpowering urge to run away.

How could this happen? some of our parents asked us near the end. We knew what they were really asking, and some of us found the grace to say, *It was nothing you did.*

We return to the kiss. The crowd has started to count down the minutes until Craig and Harry hit the twenty-four-hour mark.

Not everyone is counting. There are jeers now—people from town and people from other towns who have come to protest, who've come to yell, who've come to break whatever spell that two boys kissing can cast. Some of them make a production of praying for Craig's and Harry's souls. Some hold hastily scrawled posters: ADAM AND EVE NOT ADAM AND STEVE, HOMOSEXUALITY IS A SIN, YOU CAN'T KISS YOUR WAY OUT OF HELL. Some have brought their children.

The police don't know what to do—separate everyone into two camps or let them mingle? It takes only one shoving match for the separation to start. But the protestors will not be hidden. They want to be within hearing range of the cameras, of the boys.

The ring around the boys holds on. When someone needs to

leave, whether to go home or just go to the bathroom, another person takes his or her place. They keep their backs to the protestors, their eyes on Craig and Harry.

Tariq has now been awake for almost thirty hours. His body is wracked with caffeine, his eyes blurred by so much screen time. People keep telling him to go home, take a nap, but he doesn't want to miss a moment. If Craig and Harry are going to stay awake, he'll stay awake, too. Solidarity.

He keeps thinking of Walt Whitman, of two boys together clinging. He wonders what Whitman would make of all this. He's kept Whitman's bust on the table next to him, watching over the scene.

Craig and Harry can hear the jeering, the rumble of antipathy, but they can't hear it very clearly. Tariq offered to get them headphones to block it all out, but they're sticking to the speakers, sticking to the playlist. It helps to have words to reach for, an element of unpredictability.

The day is getting warmer. Harry signals for the removal of his hoodie, but even after it's off, he's still hot. Sweating. Craig can feel it, too—the blush rising from Harry's skin, the dampness of his shirt. What he doesn't feel is how much Harry's legs are killing him. No matter how he shifts and kicks, he can't get them to feel normal. The ache is becoming unbearable, like someone is twisting each and every vein around each and every muscle. He tries to think of other things, but pain is the loudest broadcast.

He's brought back by the *twenty-nineteen-eighteen* of a countdown. He feels Craig smile under his lips. *Seventeen-sixteen-fifteen.* People are pressing in to see. It's getting hotter and hotter. *Fourteen-thirteen-twelve.* He tries to focus. *Eleven. Ten.*

Nine. Tariq calls out that there are over three hundred thousand people watching online. *Eight. Seven. Six.* One of the news stations burns them with their lights, wants to capture this moment. *Five. Four. Three.* Craig is kissing him now. Really kissing him. Like when they were together. *Two.* It is so hot. The lights are so bright. *One.* An enormous wave of cheering.

They have made it to twenty-four hours. They have made it for a day.

Amid the wild press of celebration, Harry starts to pass out.

At exactly the same moment, Avery pulls into Ryan's driveway. Ryan is already outside waiting for him, smiling as he arrives. Avery parks the car, turns off the motor. But before he can get out of the car, Ryan jumps in.

"Let's go," Ryan says.

"Could I go inside for a sec?" Avery asks. "I have to pee."

"We'll find someplace*else," Ryan tells him. "I promise, it won't be long."

Avery doesn't want to explain that it's much easier for him to use a private bathroom than a public one. Especially in a town like Kindling. So he drives, all the time wondering why Ryan doesn't want him inside his house.

"I have a plan," Ryan says. "Are you up for a plan?"

Avery nods.

"Okay. But first, a bathroom." He tells Avery to turn left, then right. They get to a strip mall road, and Ryan indicates a McDonald's coming up. "That work?"

Avery pulls in. "You hungry?"

"Not yet. Not unless you're hungry. I just figured you could pee here."

Again, Avery doesn't want to explain. So he gets out of the car, heads inside. He feels eyes on him as he goes over to the men's room. People behind the counter glaring because he hasn't bought anything. People at tables staring because they know where he's going, know what he's doing. Nobody has to be watching for Avery to feel watched. He is almost used to it, but will never truly get used to it. The feeling that he's trespassing. The feeling that he will be confronted. The feeling that the world is full of people who think *different* is synonymous with *wrong*.

No matter how strong Avery gets, there will always be this subterranean fear, this nagging shame. We want to whisper to him that the only way to free yourself from shame is to realize how completely arbitrary it is—just what he was saying a day ago. *Stupid arbitrary shit.* He needs to take those words to heart. There is power in saying, *I am not wrong. Society is wrong.* Because there is no reason that men and women should have separate bathrooms. There is no reason that we should ever be ashamed of our bodies or ashamed of our love. We are told to cover ourselves up, hide ourselves away, so that other people can have control over us, can make us follow their rules. It is a bastardization of the concept of morality, this rule of shame. Avery should be able to walk into any restroom, any restaurant, without any fear, without any hesitation.

He is relieved that it's a one-stall bathroom, that he can lock the door and have privacy. He is embarrassed by his relief, uncomfortable with the fact that he's so uncomfortable. Ryan remains oblivious in the car. Avery envies that, and is also annoyed by it.

On the way out, the eyes are still there, the extra self-consciousness. Avery won't let it change his actions, not anymore. But he can't deny it's there. It's always there.

We didn't lose our fear until we didn't have anything left. But we still feel fear for other people.

When Avery gets back to the car, Ryan is texting with some of his friends.

"Everyone wants to meet you," Ryan says. This fills Avery with another kind of anxiety.

"Everyone?" he asks.

"I may have told one or two or seven of my friends about you. I mean, they saw us dancing the other night. I had to keep them updated."

Avery starts the car and asks, "Where to?"

"Do you want to meet some of my friends?"

The answer is yes, and the answer is no. The answer is that Avery wants to see more of Ryan's life, for sure. And the answer is that he likes it just being the two of them for now.

"Maybe later?"

"Oh, definitely later. I just need to know whether to put them on standby or not. But we've got hours of us-time to spend before that."

Avery likes the sound of this. But he still feels uneasy. Not because Ryan's making him feel wrong. Maybe he's just uneasy because nothing is easy. Unease is the natural state.

* * *

Cooper is driving his car around to recharge his phone's battery. He wants to go back on the hunt, see if maybe he can find someone better than the guy from last night. One last chance. One last time.

He goes back to the Starbucks and sits in a corner so no one can see the screen. It's just past noon on a Sunday, but the sex sites are full of people, full of come-ons. He's got ten messages from last night, people he ignored while he was chatting with Antimatter.

It's all so boring. He feels like he's spent his life looking at these faces, even though he's only had this app for a couple of months.

Twinkhunter's the one who pushes him over the edge. He's blocked this guy at least ten times. But the guy just creates a new profile and starts sending messages again. *You're so cute. You're so hot. I think we'd have a great time.* The guy looks like he works in a bank. He's got a shirtless photo even though he's too old to have a shirtless photo.

Before, Cooper's just hit the block key. This time, though, he types back.

You're disgusting.

Twinkhunter responds:

You into that?

And Cooper doesn't care anymore. Why the fuck does he have to be polite to people like this?

You are nothing more than a desperate, pathetic pedophile.

Within ten seconds, Twinkhunter's blocked him.

Cooper likes the way that feels. So he goes on.

He tells the guys who want "masculine only" that they're

just as bad as homophobes, trying to make *masculine* into some macho gym ideal.

He tells the guys who say "whites only" that they're racist scum.

He tells the sixty-year-olds who are looking for "under 18s" that they are pedophiles.

He tells the younger guys with naked pics that they should stop prostituting themselves.

You're pathetic, he writes.

You're desperate.

Are you afraid to show your face? Is that why you show your dick?

Does your boyfriend know you do this?

I think there's something wrong with my screen. I can't tell if that's your ass or your face.

You're looking for a good time? Do you really think you'll find it here?

They all start blocking him. Just like that, they disappear from his phone, disappear from his life. Antimatter isn't on right now, but Cooper feels that if he were, he'd easily find a way to get blocked there, too.

There's one guy, thirty-four, who says he's *long-term-relationship oriented.* Cooper writes back, *How long-term do you think these relationships are? Two hours? Three? If you want to find a husband, maybe you should stop looking for someone to fuck.*

Cooper figures he'll get blocked in record time. But the guy, whose screen name is TZ, writes back:

Why are you so angry?

Cooper responds, *I'm not angry. I'm just truthful.*

TZ doesn't buy it. *Who hurt you?* he asks. *Do you need help?*

Cooper blocks him right away. No way to undo it. Gone.

He takes down another Daddy looking for a Son, another Son looking for a Daddy, telling them this is no way to find family. He finds the guy from a week ago who suggested they meet in a park. He tells him to be there in fifteen minutes. Then, when the guy says he's on his way, he blocks him. Let him wonder.

Cooper's enjoying himself. Because every time he's blocked, a new face appears. It's like an endless source of desperate discontent. (Yes, there are some guys who look perfectly happy and have a sense of humor about the whole thing, but Cooper ignores them.) Five miles away. Fifteen miles away. Thirty.

He could go on for hours. But the app is on to him. There must be complaints. Because suddenly a message pops up telling him his account has been suspended. He's been frozen. Shut out for bad behavior. On a sex site.

Fine, he thinks. He deletes the account. Deletes the app.

It's too easy. He heads over to another app and starts doing the same thing. They suspend him in a matter of minutes. He deletes his profile.

He heads to Facebook. Instead of his "friends," he decides to go after pop stars and politicians. He posts links to gay porn on Justin Bieber's page. He posts links to Nazi groups on the page for a Republican congressman who compared rape to bad weather. For Taylor Swift's page, he finds a video of a sheep being decapitated.

It only takes two and a half minutes before his profile is killed. That part of his life is over.

He gets kicked out of every site he's ever created a profile on.

A block on each and every one. Stacked up, these blocks make a wall. Him on one side. The rest of the world on the other. It might be his most successful barrier yet.

It only takes an hour in a Starbucks for him to abandon his virtual life. Which is, if he's honest, most of his real life, too.

One by one he deletes his contacts, until his phone is blank. *What's left?* he asks himself.

The answer is a satisfying *nothing*.

Craig thought at least his mother would come for the twenty-four-hour mark. But the fact that she's not here means that maybe she's not watching. Maybe she doesn't know it's been a full day. Or maybe she does, and has decided to stay away.

With a couple minutes left, Craig turns his thoughts back to Harry. Sweaty, sticky Harry. From the way he shifts and tenses, Craig knows he's hurting. But he's not going to back down, and Craig loves him for it. Genuinely loves him. At this point, he's not even sure where Harry's body ends and his own body begins. At this point, even their souls have become a Venn diagram, and the overlapping space grows and grows. Forget the togetherness of dating, the togetherness of sex. This is something higher. A piece of them has stopped being *together* and started to be *the same*.

The countdown begins. Craig wants Harry to know what he's feeling. Craig wants to kiss him and mean it. They may be weary, they may be broken up, but he wants them to always have this. No matter what happens after, he wants them to be at one for this. He kisses Harry as the numbers trickle down, as the second day begins. He feels so close to Harry, and then all of a sudden he can feel Harry slipping away. As the crowd goes crazy, Harry goes slack. Craig grabs him tighter, feels the edges of their lips separating, but keeps the middle there, keeps their lips together even as Harry isn't responding. He squeezes harder, and Harry reacts. As a matter of instinct, Harry begins to turn his head, but Craig stays on top of him. Harry's eyelids flutter open, and Craig, propping him up, makes the sign for water. Harry is burning up now. The crowd doesn't understand; the crowd is still cheering. But Tariq knows. Smita knows. Harry's parents know. Craig can see it in their eyes, in their rush to get Harry water.

Harry is back on his feet now, wincing. He drinks some water through a straw, as Craig's lips seal their mouths shut. But Harry's still too hot. He needs air. He starts pulling up his shirt, exposing his skin. But it's a T-shirt. Stupidly, he wore a T-shirt. So there's no way to get it off.

Mr. and Mrs. Ramirez are at his side, asking questions.

Is he all right?

He signals yes. Because he knows what will happen if he signals no.

Is he hot?

Yes.

Does he need his shirt off?

Yes.

Will he be okay without a shirt?

Yes.

Mrs. Ramirez heads off for a second. The crowd has now realized that something's going on. The cheering has stopped, and the jeering can be heard behind it.

Someone's offering to get a fan, but Harry can't wait. His mother comes back with a scissors and asks him if he's sure.

Yes.

She hands over the scissors and he awkwardly starts cutting the back of his shirt. Right down the middle. And when it's been bisected, the two boys choreograph its delicate removal. For the first time in twenty-four hours, Craig's hands must sit lifeless at his side. Their lips are their only point of contact. It makes Craig feel distant, fragile.

As soon as the shirt is off, Harry feels better. The fan, when it comes, brings more relief.

Craig returns his hands to Harry's shoulders, his back. The heat of his skin, the slick of his sweat. Harry moves his arm around Craig, too. He moves his hand under the back of Craig's shirt. Skin on skin. Dizzying.

For a moment there, Tariq thought it was over. Staring at the screen, he didn't dare to breathe. As if holding his breath could prevent Harry's lips from slipping from Craig's. But we feel this connection all the time, don't we? Our bodies don't have to be touching to be connected to one another. Our heart races without contact. Our breath holds until the threat is gone.

"What is it?"

Neil walks into Peter's bedroom and sees a deep look of concern on his face.

Peter gestures to the screen. "It looked for a second like Harry was going to pass out. Now they're cutting off his shirt."

"Who's Harry?"

"From the kiss." Peter now points to one of the boys on the screen. "Harry. Haven't you been watching?"

"I've been doing other things."

"Well, it's getting pretty intense."

Neil knows that this is the moment to tell Peter what happened with his family, how things feel a little different now. But Peter's too focused on the boys on the screen, isn't asking him how his morning was. And Neil is still piecing his reaction together—he doesn't want Peter's take on the situation until he has his own. Or at least that's what he tells himself, to justify staying silent. The truth is, Peter will understand, but only up to a point. Peter has never had to have such a conversation with his parents. Peter has never felt like an outsider in his own house. He might claim there were moments he has. But he hasn't really. Not from Neil's point of view.

"It looks like he's rallying," Peter says. "It's been twenty-four hours. Only eight more to go."

Neil gets closer. He's looking at the kiss, yes. But his eye naturally goes to Harry's torso.

In 1992, when over two hundred thousand of us were infected and over ten thousand had died, Calvin Klein launched a new ad campaign with a white rapper named Marky Mark. If you are young and you are male, most conceptions you have of your bodily ideal can be traced to those advertisements. Every Hollister model that calls out to you, every voice in your head that tells you that abs need "definition," every ounce of the Abercrombie myth can be traced directly to Marky Mark. Whether you subscribe to these ideals or reject them, they are the unrealistic standard you must face. It's what's being sold to you.

Harry's torso is not like this. It dares to be a regular body as it is broadcast out among all the ideals. He is neither fat nor thin. There is a line of hair from his chest to his jeans. His stomach is not taut. You cannot see his abs.

In other words, he reminds us of the way we were as teenagers, the way we were before the world set in.

Why is Marky Mark smiling in those ads? It's not just that he has a perfect body. No, it's as if he knows that soon enough, our bodies will be broadcast. Soon enough, our images will enter the ether. Everyone will want to look like him, because they will feel like they are being looked at all the time.

Harry, of course, knows he is being looked at. But what he looks like is the farthest thing from his mind. When your body starts to turn against you—when the surface value of the skin is nothing compared to the fireworks of pain in your muscles and your bones—the supposed truth of beauty falls away, because there are more important concerns to attend to.

Believe us. We know this.

* * *

Avery wonders why Ryan is looking at him out of the corner of his eye, why Ryan would rather watch him than watch the road. Even when friends look at Avery, a small part of him still worries they are looking for flaws, irregularities. In this, Avery isn't all that different from anyone else. We all worry that looking *at* is really looking *for*.

Finally, Avery can't stand it. The look. Then a knowing smile. Then another look.

"What?" he asks.

This only makes Ryan smile more. "I'm sorry," he says. "I don't usually like people. So when I do, part of me is really amused and the other part refuses to believe it's happening."

Maybe this is why we like watching you so much. Everything is still new to you. We are long past the experience, although we witness new things all the time. But you. New is not just a fact. New can be an emotion.

"What are we doing?" Avery asks. It is not meant as an existential question. He just wants to know what they're doing next.

"I figured we'd start with pancakes. Do you want pancakes?"

"It's hard to imagine a scenario where someone would say no to pancakes."

So they go to the pancake house. Because it's a small town, Avery notices Ryan checking out who else is inside before committing to a table.

"Looking for anyone in particular?"

Ryan smiles again. "No. Just habit, I guess."

"How many people are in your high school?"

"About two hundred. You?"

"Eighty."

"You must stick out. I mean, with the pink hair and all."

"I bet you blend right in."

"Trying to blend in would be like being put through a blender. I abstain."

Avery finds this funny. "What did you just say?"

"I said, 'I abstain.'"

"Is that what you say when the popular kids try to get you to hang out with them? 'I'm sorry, but I abstain from blending in. There are just too many perks to being a wallflower.'"

"Yup. That's precisely what I say. But do they stop? No. The popular kids keep bugging me. Calling. Texting. Showing up on my doorstep. Begging like dogs. I'm embarrassed for them."

"I know *precisely* how you feel."

To emphasize his point, Avery squeezes Ryan's hand. It's such an openly lame excuse to touch him, and both of them smile in acknowledgment of this.

"Part of you is amused," Avery says. "And part of you doesn't believe this is happening."

Ryan nods. "And in the Pancake Century Diner, of all places."

"Well," Avery says, "it *is* the Pancake Century, after all."

The waitress comes to take their order. Each of them thinks about pulling his hand away, but neither of them does.

* * *

Craig thinks of pancakes. He thinks of warm maple syrup and blueberries and butter melting. He thinks of the savory smoke of bacon on his tongue. A glass of cold orange juice. He tries to conjure their taste, but taste is elusive when it comes to memory. So instead he has to rely on his memory of how they look. How they smell. How happy they make him.

He focuses back on Harry. Harry, who is fading. Craig feels awful for thinking it, but the thought is there: If they don't make it now, it will probably be because of Harry. Craig's texted over his shoulder, asked him if he's okay, and Harry keeps saying he is, keeps saying now that he's cooled down, he's back on track. But Craig can feel the lie throughout Harry's body, can touch the tight muscles, can notice all the small movements Harry is making to keep himself upright, to keep himself going.

And I was never the stronger one. Craig allows himself to say it, if only to himself. All through their relationship, Harry was the one in charge, Harry was the one who gave them direction. This wasn't because Harry was smarter or even better at it than Craig was; it just meant more to him, to be in control. And Craig didn't really care, so he ceded it away. He liked not being responsible all the time.

Complacency. Craig realizes now that this was complacency. One of the reasons he liked the sound of Harry's voice was because it meant he didn't have to use his own. But eventually this strategy backfired. Eventually Harry realized what was happening, and didn't feel right about it. He wanted Craig to fight a little more, but by the time Craig started fighting for them to stay together, he had already lost.

Now he's fighting for something different, something that feels more elemental. He's fighting to stay standing. He's fighting to go without food, without a bathroom. He's fighting to keep his lips on Harry's for seven more hours. And he's fighting to help Harry do all of these things as well.

It's one of the secrets of strength: We're so much more likely to find it in the service of others than we are to find it in service to ourselves. We have no idea why this is. It's not just the mother who lifts the car to free her child, or the guy who shields his girlfriend when the gunman starts to fire. Those are extremes, brave extremes, which life rarely calls on us to offer. No, it is the less extreme strength—a strength that is not so much situational as it is constitutional—that we will find in order to give. How often did we see this, as we were dying? How many soft-spoken lovers turned into fierce watchdogs over our care? How many reticent parents shed that reticence to be there with us? Not all. Certainly, not everyone showed strength. Some supposedly strong people in our lives showed that their strength was actually made of straw. But so many held us up in ways they would not have held themselves. They saw us through, even as their worlds crumbled through their fingers. They kept fighting, even after we were gone. Or especially because we were gone. They kept fighting for us.

We are gone, and maybe our spirits are gone, too, as the ones who knew us stop remembering us so often, or come to join us. But the spirit of that strength—it carries through. It is there for the taking. You just have to reach for it and find it, as Craig is doing now. He would never grasp at it for himself, not in this way. But for Harry, he will.

Cooper, meanwhile, refuses to grasp. He refuses to hold. He refuses to feel.

We watch him letting go, but we will not let go of him.

He is driving without realizing he is driving. He knows there is a destination out there for him, and he is working his way toward it. In the meantime, he is taking the empty census of people who love him. He is not afraid of hurting anyone, because he doesn't think anyone cares about him enough to be hurt. Surely, they will go through the motions. They will have their tears once he's left. But underneath that performance of sadness, he feels their relief. They don't want him to come back, so he won't.

Love, he thinks, is a lie that people tell each other in order to make the world bearable. He is not up for the lie anymore. And nobody is going to lie to him like that, anyway. He's not even worth a lie.

We want him to take a census of the future. We want him to consider that love does make the world bearable, but that does not make it a lie. We want him to see the time when he will feel it, truly feel it, for the first time. But the future is something he is no longer considering.

In his mind, the future is a theory that has already been proven false.

* * *

What a powerful word, *future*. Of all the abstractions we can articulate to ourselves, of all the concepts we have that other animals do not, how extraordinary the ability to consider a time that's never been experienced. And how tragic not to consider it. It galls us, we with such a limited future, to see someone brush it aside as meaningless, when it has an endless capacity for meaning, and an endless number of meanings that can be found within it.

Sing us that old refrain.
Where do you want to go?
I don't know—where do you want to go?
What do you want to do?
I don't know—what do you want to do?

The feed of the two boys kissing stays on in the background as Neil and Peter play video games in Neil's room. Peter senses something is not quite right with Neil—his heart doesn't seem into the game, and it's the game he brought over a few days ago, desperate to make it to level thirty-two by the end of the week. Peter is afraid it's still about the stupid text he got from Simon, or about something else that's them-related. So he doesn't say anything, because he knows Neil will bring it up when he's ready to bring it up. Maybe it isn't anything at all.

For his part, Neil doesn't understand why he isn't talking to Peter, why he's killing Russian assassins instead of telling Peter that his world has shifted. He's waiting for Peter to ask him what's happened, because he thinks it's clear something's happened, and why should he always have to be the one to point it out?

Peter pauses the game.

"Are you hungry?" he asks.

"Not really" is Neil's reply.

"Thirsty?"

"No."

"Do you want to do something else?"

"Do *you* want to do something else?"

"Are you in the throes of constipation?"

Neil is not in the mood for this. "No."

"Pregnant?"

"No."

"Sick of this game?"

"Which game?"

"The one you're playing."

"Which one am I playing?"

"The one on the screen right now. *Balkan Bloodbath 12*."

"Oh. No. I'm fine."

Here's where Peter should say it. *What's going on?*

But instead he unpauses the game.

"If you're fine," he says, "I'm fine."

They continue to play.

Ryan hasn't had to spend much time thinking about where to take Avery next, because already they are running out of cool places in Kindling. If they're not on the river or at Aunt Caitlin's or in the Pancake Century Diner, there are very few places worth exploring. The Kindling Café is the one that's left, but that's where everyone is. He wants Avery to meet his friends, but not yet. He still wants them to be alone together, with no one watching, no one even noticing. This is Ryan's relationship to this town: He doesn't really want to leave any marks, and he wants Kindling to leave as few marks as possible on him. He knows he's been defined by this town. And, of course, the more he's tried to resist definition, the more they've defined him. But this—this time with Avery—needs to exist outside definition. Or, at the very least, he and Avery need to get a chance to define it themselves.

So he directs Avery to Mr. Footer's, the old relic of a miniature golf course. It's been closed for years now, but no one's bought the land, so it sits in its abandoned state, nearly postapocalyptic in its decay. There's a lock on the gates, but the gates themselves have worn away in places, making it easy to come and go. At night it's a breeding ground for stoners and crankheads, but during the day it's graveyard quiet.

"Where exactly are you taking me?" Avery asks. Ryan has a flash of seeing the site through his eyes, and realizes this might be a mistake. But he doesn't want to turn back now.

He tells Avery to park in front. "When I was a kid," he explains, "this place was the best place around. Like, if you were really good and did all your chores, Mom and Dad would take you here. You'd play all the mini golf you could, and then there'd be ice cream and video games in the hut over there after."

Avery takes it all in. "So what happened?"

Ryan shrugs. "One day it was here, and then the next day there was a sign saying it was over. It's sat here ever since, abandoned."

"And do you come here often?"

"Only with *special* people."

"Oh, gee. I'm so flattered," Avery deadpans. But in a way, he *is* flattered. Had Ryan driven over to Marigold, Avery would have been forced to take him to a T.G.I. Friday's or a movie. This is definitely not that.

"Let's go," Ryan says. They leave the car and crawl through a gap in the gate. Inside, everything is broken. Toppled windmills, fetid moats, bottles left smashed and cans left crushed.

"Want to play?" Avery asks.

Ryan looks at the torn-up greens. The holes filled with cigarette butts.

"I'm not sure that will work," he says. "There aren't any clubs anymore. Or golf balls."

"So?"

"So . . . it's hard to play mini golf without those things."

"Use your imagination," Avery says, walking to the base of the first green and putting down an invisible ball. "This is the most amazing mini-golf course ever created. For example, this hole is patrolled by live alligators. If they swallow your ball, it's three strokes. If they swallow you, it's five."

Avery takes an exaggerated swing with a nonexistent club, then makes a production of watching the ball soar into the air and drop to the green. "Comeoncomeoncomeon," he murmurs. Then he sighs. "Not a hole in one, but at least I dodged the gators. Your turn."

Ryan walks over and puts down his own invisible ball. "I hope you don't mind that I took the pink one," he says.

"I don't mind at all."

Ryan swings at the ball. They both watch it rise and fall.

"Not bad," Avery says.

"At least I didn't hit a gator."

Ryan thinks Avery will stop then, will want to leave this desolate place. But he heads right over to where his ball is and makes the putt, then steps out of the way for Ryan's turn. Ryan follows his lead, but misses the shot. He gets the next one in.

Avery makes a gesture of gathering the golf balls, then walks to the next hole.

"Your turn," he says. "What's the story?"

The story Ryan tells is that this green is riddled with troughs of chocolate; if your ball falls in, it will taste better, but will also slow you down. And actually, the golf ball is no longer a ball. It's a golf-ball-size gobstopper.

The story Ryan *feels* is a different matter. The story Ryan feels is the one that's being written with each minute, this confounding and enjoyable story of the two of them finding a good time in what he now sees is a remarkably dire place. He's always appreciated how derelict it was, but that was when he was feeling pretty derelict himself. In the past couple of years, there was some catharsis in seeing his childhood so visibly trashed, as if there was some confirmation here about what growing up should feel like.

But with Avery, a little of that old wonder returns. Ryan plays along, and it's a relief to be playing. By the fifth hole they're not even golfing anymore; they're just describing all the things they don't really see. Avery erects the Taj Mahal on hole five, and Ryan presents the world's first antigravity mini golf on hole six. At hole seven, they start walking hand in hand, surveyors of an imaginary landscape. Instead of solemnly holding hands, they swing them back and forth, stretch out and pull back together. The sun isn't shining, but they don't notice. If anyone were to ask them later, they'd swear that it was.

It is not as simple as Ryan looking at Avery and feeling they've known each other forever. In fact, it doesn't feel like that at all. Ryan feels like he is just getting to know Avery, and that getting to know Avery isn't going to be like getting to know anyone else he's ever gotten to know.

There's a wishing well in the middle of the ninth hole. This is not imaginary—it is sitting there, largely intact from its glory days. Avery reaches into his pocket and pulls out a penny.

"No," Ryan finds himself saying. "Don't."

Avery shoots him a quizzical look. "Don't?"

"I've thrown pennies in that well all my life. And not a single wish has ever come true."

As a kid he wished for money or fame or toys or friends. More recent wishes were for so many other things, all of them synonymous with love or escape.

He worries he's ruined it now, by suddenly being serious. That's always been his problem, his inability to live in false worlds for that long.

Avery doesn't ask him what he wished for. He doesn't need to.

"Here," he says. "Maybe you didn't do it right."

Avery takes the penny and moves it to Ryan's lips. Ryan holds there, not really knowing what's happening. Then Avery leans in and kisses him, kisses him so that they are both kissing the penny. When he pulls back, the penny falls, and he catches it in his palm.

"Now make a wish," he says.

And Ryan thinks, *I want to be happy.*

"Got it?" Avery asks.

Ryan nods, and Avery tosses the penny into the well. They both listen, but neither hears it land. Then Avery returns to him, comes closer again, and now they are kissing with nothing between them. Lips closed, then lips open. Hands empty, then hands entwined.

A minute or two of this, then Avery pulls back and says, "We're only half done!"

They walk, fingers still woven together, to the tenth hole.

"It's a cloud," Ryan says. "The whole thing is a cloud."

They become so caught in their discussion of golfing within clouds that they don't hear the footsteps, don't hear the laughter coming their way. Then the voices are too loud to ignore.

Ryan turns and sees who's coming.

"What?" Avery asks.

And Ryan says, "Oh shit."

Harry is crying. He is in so much pain that he's started to cry. His legs are seizing up, and his bladder feels like it's full of rocks, and he isn't choosing to cry, but his eyes are crying nonetheless. He's lost control of them. He's lost control of everything, except for his lips. All of the control that he has left, he has to put there. Even as his body is shouting *surrender*. Even as his mind is telling him there is no way to last another five hours.

There are four of them. Avery has no idea who they are, and neither do we, but just like us, Avery has some idea of where this is going. It's the sneering looks, the swagger in the walk, the almost aimless spite in their laughter. It's a particular brand of asshole, easily found in teenage boys traveling in packs.

"What's up, Ryan?" one of them taunts. "Who's your *boyfriend*?"

Ryan lets go of Avery's hand.

"What do you want, Skylar?" he says.

"We saw a car out front. What are you boys up to?"

Avery sees now that Skylar and one of the other guys are holding golf clubs. Skylar sees him looking and smiles. Then he spots a bottle on the ground and swings the club, knocking the bottle in Ryan and Avery's direction. Ryan doesn't flinch, but Avery does.

We don't need to tell you what Skylar's like, do we? You must already know. In the big scheme of things, he's a powerless cog. So he exerts as much power as he can in any situation he can dominate. He tries to build his self-worth on the backs of others, and it works a little, but never enough. It doesn't make him any smarter. It doesn't give him more of a future. It gives him the same instant gratification as sex or drugs. He doesn't hate Ryan, not really. He just sees in him an opportunity to be in control. Especially with an audience.

Ryan tries to stay away from him—tries to stay away from all of them. Because there are always more of them, and because if he fights them, he's going to have to fight them every day after that, whereas if he manages to avoid them, ultimately he will disappear altogether. Or that's what he's told himself—that's what we always told ourselves. Do not engage. Do not make it worse. Walk away. Not run away—don't be a coward, don't let them see your fear. *Walk* away.

If Avery wasn't here, that's what he'd be doing. Tell them to have a fun game, then walk away like he was handing over the course to them. But there's no getting away with that now. It's more fun for Skylar to go for the kill with Avery watching.

Skylar lines up another bottle, and this time it smashes on impact, glass flying everywhere. The other guys find this hilarious.

Avery can feel himself shutting down, going into survival mode.

"What the fuck do you guys want?" Ryan spits out.

"So tough!" Skylar mocks. Then he throws his golf club at Ryan's face.

Or at least he makes it look like he's going to throw the golf club at Ryan's face. At the last possible moment, he holds on to it. But not before Ryan's lifted up his arm, cringed from the blow that never comes.

Avery can see Ryan's humiliation at falling for the fakeout. As the guys are laughing some more, Avery wants to walk over and put a comforting hand on Ryan's back, wants to tell him it's okay. But he can't do that, because he's not sure what kind of reaction that will get, and also he's not sure if it really is okay.

What Avery doesn't know is that Ryan's humiliation isn't just from the moment, but is the accumulation of abuse from Skylar and other guys like Skylar. They've trespassed all over his life, spit and stomped and sabotaged any degree of safety or comfort he'd managed to build. This is the true tyranny—not the actual taunts or shoves, but the exhaustion that comes from living with it for so long, so relentlessly.

It killed us, to be picked on, to be ridiculed for being something we weren't even allowed to be. So many of us first heard the word *gay* as an insult, an abomination. So many of us were called a faggot before we even knew what that meant. Not all of us—some of us hid so deep that no one could find our weakness. Some of us were bullies ourselves in order to cover our tracks, or because we hated what we were so much that we had to attack it in other people. A lot of us had to suffer at the hands of people who were dumber and/or meaner than we were, just because they were bigger, just because they were louder, just because of who their fathers were or what team they were on, or because they had the sheer nerve to kick us around while we didn't have the defenses to fight back.

There was always a time before we were marked. For Ryan, there's a time that he played Little League with Skylar. Their mothers even carpooled. But that history means nothing here.

"Did we interrupt you guys making out?" Skylar says with a playful disgust. "Did we miss the show?" He's close now, too close. He takes the golf club and uses it to push Avery toward Ryan. "Don't let us stop you. Let's see what you've got."

Avery feels the guys' eyes on him and has no idea what they see.

"Come on!" one of the guys calls out. "Do it!"

Ryan is coiled with anger, but he can't uncoil it into action. Not until Skylar starts to poke him with the golf club, making rude kissing noises. It's too much. Ryan grabs at the club, tries to pull it out of Skylar's hands. He expects Skylar to pull back, but instead Skylar surprises Ryan by pushing instead. Ryan's caught off balance and falls back on his ass, knocking into Avery. *Then* Skylar pulls back on the club, easily shifting it out of Ryan's hand.

Everyone is staring at Ryan on the ground, even Avery. The other guys are loving it, laying on the insults. But Skylar stays quiet. He lets his satisfaction speak for him. No matter what Ryan does now, Skylar's already won.

"You need to get a new boyfriend," he tells Avery. "This one's damaged."

"Fuck you," Avery says. It feels lame to say it. Stupid. There has to be something better for him to say, but that's all he's got.

"No," Skylar says. "Fuck *you.*"

Ryan is getting up now. Skylar steps back and putts a piece of glass so it hits Ryan's sneaker.

"Let's go," Avery says.

"What, so soon?" Skylar taunts. "That wasn't much of a show!"

Avery tries to read the expression in Ryan's eyes, but he can't. He has no idea what Ryan is thinking right now, what he's going to do next. It's like none of the rest of them are there—it's just Ryan and Skylar, facing off.

"I want to go," Avery says. Let them blame him. Let him be the weak one, if that will get them out of here.

"Okay," Ryan says. It's directed at Avery, but he doesn't take his eyes off Skylar. "It was great to see you guys."

"Yeah, fag, great to see you, too," Skylar replies.

Ryan and Avery start to walk away. The guys respond by knocking more cans and bottles in their direction. Ryan doesn't break into a run. He just keeps walking, and Avery keeps pace. Glass and aluminum are hitting them, flying all around them. The guys are whooping with joy. They follow for a short distance, then finally, at the sixth hole, let them go. Ryan despises how thankful he is for this.

As soon as they are out of range, safely crawling back through the opening in the gate, the cork pops on all the words Avery has been keeping inside. "That was scary," he says. "But we're fine. We're totally fine. Those guys are assholes. The important thing is that we're okay. Let's just forget about it, because there's no use in worrying about it now. We're okay, right?"

"I'm really sorry," Ryan says, "but I think I need us to be quiet for a second."

He tries to say it gently, tries to make it clear that it's nothing personal against Avery, but Avery can't help but feel a little rebuked.

Skylar's parked his car so that it's blocking Avery's. And it's a truck, so it's not like Avery can ram his way out. Instead Avery has to do a twenty-point turn and run over a sidewalk to get out. The whole time, Ryan seethes.

"It's all right," Avery says.

"No, it's *not*," Ryan snaps.

Avery finishes the maneuvering and gets them out of the parking lot.

"What's next?" he asks.

Ryan knows he needs to extricate himself from what just happened, needs to step outside of it and return to the day that he and Avery were having. But the rage he's feeling is volcanic. If Avery weren't here, he'd be going back there with a golf club of his own. He'd wait until they weren't looking, and then he'd beat the hell out of them. Or at least that's what he wants to tell himself. These scenarios are much clearer when they're not actually happening.

"Ryan?"

Ryan hasn't heard Avery's question, and doesn't realize that Avery needs to know where they're going. He looks at his watch and realizes he told Alicia they'd drop by in about fifteen minutes.

"Make a left," he says.

Avery wants to ask more, but settles into patience instead. *Let it out*, he wants to tell Ryan. *Say what you need to say.*

But Ryan's not there yet. He can't say it out loud. And he can't let it go.

Cooper goes to McDonald's to get something to eat and realizes he doesn't have that much money left. This should bother him, but it doesn't. He barely even notices it.

Instead he sits at a corner table and eats his Quarter Pounder. People talk and laugh and push around him, but he stares off into a space that isn't there, his thoughts as anonymous as his surroundings. He finishes the burger in six minutes, then sits around for another thirty. Playing things out in his mind. Talking to himself because there is no one else to talk to.

Death is hard, and facing death is painful. But even more painful is the feeling that no one cares. To not have a friend in the world. Some of us died surrounded by loved ones. Some of us had loved ones who couldn't make it in time, who were too far away or just off getting some sleep. But there are also those of us who can tell you what it's like to have no one who you love, no one who loves you. It is very hard to stay alive just for your own sake. It is very hard to stare into day after day after day without another familiar face staring back. It turns your heart into a purposeless muscle.

The fewer connections you have to the world, the easier it is to leave.

We need to turn back to Harry and Craig. We need to see them standing there. The day is getting warmer, and as a result, their bodies seem to give off more heat. We watch Craig's hand press against Harry's back, and we remember the miraculous feel of skin. Such a thing to miss. Touching his chest and feeling the heartbeat beneath. Touching his back and feeling his spine. Breath against our necks. The chill of pulling away. The furnace of wrapping together.

Twenty-seven hours and five minutes is a long time to kiss. So is twenty-seven hours and six minutes. Harry and Craig are conscious of everything going on around them. The sea of faces keeps altering itself, updating itself. The music runs from song to song. Mykal has become the self-designated cheerleader—if the supporters grow too quiet, he gives them a rise. After football practice ended, there was an additional buzz of dissent—not all the players, but some. But these dissenters soon grew bored. There's not much to watch when it's two boys kissing. You have to be devoted to stay.

Tariq's consciousness is warping under sleeplessness. He starts muttering Walt Whitman to keep himself going, to keep his thoughts in sequence. Smita hears him and starts to do it, too. When Mykal hears this, he turns it into a cheer.

We two boys together clinging!
One the other never leaving!
Power enjoying!
Elbows stretching!
Fingers clutching!
Arm'd and fearless!
Eating!
Drinking!
Sleeping!
Loving!

Harry and Craig hold on to each other. Each of them, in his own thoughts, in his own way, wonders, *How long can you hold on to a body?*

We want to tell them, *A long time*. They are young. They

don't understand. It is natural for another body to become as yours as your own. It is natural to have that connection, that familiarity. We are ever-regenerating beings, but we always keep the same approximation, and in this way we can be known. And held.

Hold on to his body, we want to tell each of them. And then, *Hold on to your own*.

Harry coughs. Craig takes it. He doesn't even flinch.

Neil sits next to Peter as Peter plays video games. Peter plays video games, but is mostly aware of sitting next to Neil.

Peter doesn't know what to say, so he leans. Only a few inches, but now their shoulders are touching. Now they are in some simple way together.

Avery is happy to meet Ryan's friends, but also a little at sea. It's not that Ryan doesn't introduce them, but once he does, it's like he's checked out of the conversation. His mind is still back in the mini-golf place. He is still stewing in his own helpless anger.

Ryan's best friend, Alicia, senses something is off. Avery wants to tell her, *It wasn't me. I swear it wasn't me.* But she must sense this, too, because she is extra welcoming to Avery, trying to tell him funny Ryan-growing-up stories to make him feel less isolated. In fact, of the four friends that are sitting around the table in the coffeehouse, only one of them—Dez—seems to be studying Avery a little too hard, trying to figure out what's under Avery's shirt.

Finally, Ryan tells them what happened—not every detail, but the general gist of it. Avery is relieved, figuring that this will allow Ryan to release it, get over it. Certainly, everyone's sympathetic, muttering an almost endless list of synonyms for the word *asshole* to describe Skylar and the other guys.

But it's not enough for Ryan to turn it into a story. At the end he says, "I really should have done something. Smashed up his car. Called the police to report them trespassing. Something. I mean, I guess it's not too late."

"What do you mean, 'it's not too late'?" Alicia asks, in a way that Avery doesn't feel he can.

"I mean, it's not like I don't know where he lives."

Alicia nods. But then she says, "Ryan, I get that you're mad. But I think you need to take it down a notch."

"Easy for you to say. You weren't there. Right?" With this, he looks at Avery.

Avery doesn't know exactly what he's being asked. The question appears to be whether or not Alicia was there, and they all know the answer to that. Ryan wants something more from him.

"I think you guys are much better company," Avery says, winning points from everyone but Ryan.

We see how unsatisfied Ryan is with this. With Avery. With Alicia. With all of them for not sharing his rage. We know this feeling well. There were times we were subsumed within our rage—it didn't feel like something we created, but something that was outside of us, all around us, closing in. After so many

171

years of denying our rage, denying our anger, it was powerful to acknowledge it, to allow it to fuel us, to harness the rage into outrage, taking the thing that felt outside of us and then shooting it back out from the inside.

Part of the use of anger is this acknowledgment, this harnessing. But the other part—the part that was sometimes hardest for us, especially in our pain—is the matter of aim. That is, sometimes the power of anger is so intense that you will shoot it everywhere. Even when, in truth, you should only ever shoot your anger at the people you are truly angry at, the people who truly deserve your rage. Ryan, so fixated on his hatred of Skylar, doesn't even realize that he's letting the hatred spill over, scattershot.

Alicia asks Avery about his pink hair and how long he's had it, then asks more questions about life in Marigold. Really, what she wants is for Avery to go to the restroom or outside to make a phone call, so she can get Ryan alone and tell him to remember what this day was supposed to be about, to remember how excited he was when he asked her to gather people to meet this boy who'd fallen into his life. But Avery doesn't leave the table, and Ryan goes unwarned by his best friend.

"What are you going to do now?" she asks when the conversation has run its course.

"I'm not sure," Ryan says. But she can see it, clearly. His mind is still stamped with the word *revenge*.

Neil knows what Peter is doing, leaning his shoulder in like that. He knows what Peter is saying. He doesn't move away.

But he still doesn't tell Peter what happened, and still doesn't understand why.

Cooper leaves McDonald's. Walks back into the world. Waits for night to fall.

Craig looks around the crowd for his family and doesn't see them.

Harry tries to focus on the texts and emails coming in, all the posts. He barely has the strength to hold his phone, but he types as many answers as he can, trying to lose himself in words, trying to pass the time in words.

Harry's father watches his son and feels something enormous inside of him. His own father would have never understood what he was seeing, what he was feeling. His own father would have had more than a few things to say about this. But his own father was not, in many ways, worthy of his grandson, just as Harry's father is feeling, in many ways, unworthy of his son. What he feels is more than pride. *Here,* he thinks, *is the meaning of everything.* Right here in front of him. His child.

Tom, standing right next to Mr. Ramirez, wishes we were there to see it.

We are right here, we tell him.

We are right

here.

"Is there anything you want to do?" Ryan asks when they get to Avery's car.

I want a do-over, Avery thinks. *I want the last two hours back.*

Craig sees the look on Tariq's face before he sees his own phone in Tariq's hand. For the past few hours, Craig's let Harry be the texter, let Harry be the person saying thank you to the inexplicable thousands who've been tuning in. But Tariq's expression lets him know this isn't about that. This is something else.

Tariq hands over the phone. It's a message from his brother Kevin.

Went for a drive. Good luck.

That's all. That's it.

His family isn't coming.

His family. Isn't. Coming.

At some point in the night his father must have decided. It had to have been his father.

They've left. They won't be back until it's over.

Craig feels like his skin has been ripped off from the inside. He feels that all of these people watching, all of these people can see what's happened, can see everything that's never going to happen. No reunion. No cheering section. Nothing.

The tears fall even before he thinks about them. Of all the things his body is doing, this is the one that makes the most sense. When you are sad, it makes sense for the body to want your eyes to clear quickly.

Harry still doesn't know what's happening, although he has a feeling he knows. Craig gestures to Tariq to share the message with Harry, and Harry's fears are confirmed. Now Smita and Mrs. Ramirez are also coming over, seeing something's wrong.

The crowd cheers louder, calls out the boys' names. Hundreds of voices calling out the name that Craig's parents gave him. It all sounds meaningless to him.

Something comes over Tariq. He can't stop himself from doing it. He tells Rachel to watch the computers, watch the feed, and he bolts through the crowd. This is the first time he's been away from Craig and Harry, this is the first time he's taken a break, and he doesn't know where the energy is coming from, but once he's through the press of people, he's sprinting like a gold medalist through his town. His breathing is heavy and all his old wounds feel like they're on the verge of opening, but he powers through that, pushes himself until he's on Craig's street, in Craig's driveway, running up Craig's front walk. Then he's pounding at the door—really pounding—yelling at them to come out, shouting that he knows they're in there, pleading with them to be there, to come with him, to not be this stupid, to not make this mistake. *"He needs you,"* he tells them. *"He needs you,"* he says over and over again, until his hand grows too tired of pounding and his lungs grow too tired of yelling.

The house creaks and settles, as if to tell Tariq of its own abandonment. The sun blinks under a cloud. There's not a word of response, because there's no one around to craft one.

Tariq does not cry. He does not bother the house any further. He wanted to be the one to make the wrong thing right, as so many of us do. That he's failed is almost beside the point. In the rush of everything when it's over, he will probably forget to tell Craig that he tried this, that he did this.

We tell him it was a nice try. As he walks back to the school, we try to walk beside him. We want him to feel he has company.

Craig realizes how much he was waiting for them, now that he's not waiting for them anymore.

He is also surprised to find their absence is not going to make him drown.

Harry is trying to be there for Craig. Trying so hard. Just when it feels like there can't be anything new to say in the kiss, he tries to say this. And Craig hears it. Craig starts tracing something on his back. At first Harry thinks it's a *P*, or a lowercase *e*. But it doubles on itself—a heart.

Harry responds with an exclamation point.

"You are not alone," he says, his mouth still on Craig's.

"What?" Craig asks.

"You are not alone," Harry says again.

And this time Craig hears it.

Neil leaves Peter's side, walks over to Peter's computer. The two boys are still on there, kissing. Neil leans in, tries to get a sense of their thoughts. He makes it full screen, but that only makes them blurrier.

"We should go there," he finds himself saying. "Do you think your mom will give us a ride?"

"I just want to drive past," Ryan says. "To see if they're still there."

Avery wants to refuse. But instead he silently complies as Ryan tells him to turn left, to turn right.

There it is again. The abandoned mini golf.

The truck is gone.

Avery can't tell if Ryan is disappointed or relieved. Maybe both.

"I think I know where they might be," he says. He tells Avery to pull out and make a left.

Avery makes it through two green lights. When a red light stops them at the third intersection and Ryan says to take another left, Avery decides he's neither going to give in or give up. Instead he's going to give Ryan one last chance.

Ryan's confused when Avery shifts to the right lane and makes a right turn. Even more so when Avery pulls over into the parking lot of a law office.

"What are you doing?" he asks Avery.

And Avery says, "You're ruining it. You have to stop now before you ruin it completely."

Cooper pulls his car onto the highway. He is leaving his town for good. He doesn't give it a second thought. He doesn't feel anyone there deserves a goodbye.

Only two hours to go.

More camera crews, more protestors. More heat, more noise.

For all the booster shots of caffeine, Craig wants sleep as badly as he wants to sit down. He tries to keep his mind from slipping into the bad questions, but at this point, he's somewhat defenseless against them. All of his unspoken, even unacknowledged, reasons for doing this are falling away. Didn't he think it would bring his family together around him? Didn't he think they'd be proud? And wasn't Smita right—didn't he think this would get Harry back, make them a couple again? And what about what happened to Tariq—did he really think this would somehow correct that, would prevent such things from ever happening again? If anything, isn't he making it worse, giving a reason for the camera crews to sell the other side's hate into the airwaves?

Why are you doing this? he asks himself, and with all the other answers falling away, he's not sure what's left. We could tell him, but he has to figure it out for himself. We know that. It's impossible for us to arm him against despair. He must arm himself.

Harry is so hot. He's been making the *W* sign for water, has been drinking what feels to be so much of it. (It's really just half a bottle.) And now he has to pee so badly. But all these people are watching. All of these people are here. He can't imagine taking a pee break in front of them. This is the ultimate pee shy. He tries to hold it in. It's painful.

The police are blocking off the street now. The whole force is out, but there aren't really that many of them. There's no way to screen everyone coming in. Any fool could bring a gun. Anyone who wanted to stop the kiss could.

Most of the people who are coming at this point are like the two who step out of Peter's mom's car. While there's no short-age of protestors, most of the people who are migrating here are doing so because they feel some connection to the kiss. In their actions, Craig and Harry are saying the thing that they want to say. So they find themselves hopping on buses, getting into cars. They find themselves at the Millburn train station, where a helpful old woman tells them how to walk on over to the high school, and not to confuse it with the middle school, which is much closer. Now that there are less than two hours left, there's an excitement buzzing through the yard when Peter and Neil get there. They're astonished to see all the people, to see the wall of friends that is protecting Craig and Harry from the pro-testors, from any threat that may come. In the throng, Craig and Harry are just two bodies curving into an A. They are the steady center of a wider celebration, the first and tightest ripple.

Peter and Neil pause at the outskirts to get the lay of the land. Or at least that's why Peter pauses, to get a sense of where everyone else is and to see if he knows anyone there. Neil pauses to look at Peter—to really look at him and ask himself what he wants. He knows he loves Peter, and also knows he's not sure what that means. There is no one else in the world that he wants to kiss or screw or talk to or share his life with. So why, he wonders, does a part of it still feel empty? Why, after a year, isn't it complete?

He's on the verge of it—we can tell. He is on the verge of finding that very hard truth—that it will never be complete, or feel complete. This is usually something you only have to learn once—that just like there is no such thing as forever, there is no such thing as total. When you're in the thrall of your first love, this discovery feels like the breaking of all momentum, the undermining of all promise. For the past year, Neil has assumed that love was like a liquid pouring into a vessel, and that the longer you loved, the more full the vessel became, until it was entirely full. The truth is that over time, the vessel expands as well. You grow. Your life widens. And you can't expect your partner's love alone to fill you. There will always be space for other things. And that space isn't empty as much as it's filled by another element. Even though the liquid is easier to see, you have to learn to appreciate the air.

We didn't learn this all at once. Some of us didn't learn it at all, or learned it and then forgot it as things became really bad. But for all of us, there was a moment like this—the record skips, and you have the chance to either switch away from the song or to let it play through, a little more flawed than before.

"Look at all these people," Peter says to Neil. "Look at this!"

Neil looks at him and sees a big nerdy goofball. He looks at him and sees someone whose mom would drive him here and will pick them up later. He looks at him and sees maybe not his future, but definitely his present.

When Neil tells Peter what happened at his house this morning, as he will in about forty seconds, Peter will at first be confused and hurt that Neil didn't tell him right away. Neil will see this, but won't apologize. Within another five minutes, Peter won't really care, because he'll want to know everything that happened, will want to be there with Neil, even after the fact, to give support. He'll hug Neil into him, and Neil will hug him right back, and more love will flow into each of the vessels, and each of the vessels will expand a little bit more.

181

"Ruining it?" Ryan says. When he starts the first word, he genuinely doesn't understand what Avery means, but by the time he hits the question mark, he does. So before Avery can answer he says, "Oh. Yeah."

"I want to get the day back," Avery says.

And Ryan, defensive, replies, "I wasn't the one who took it away."

As soon as he says this, we know Ryan has to make a decision, and that it's an important one. Because if he makes the wrong decision here, the odds are good that he will keep making it. Those of us who died angry can recognize the pattern. It is unfair that Ryan needs to make this choice—he is absolutely correct that the day was taken away from him. But now it's in his power to get it back. Only he'll need to get past his anger in order to do so.

Avery doesn't know the stakes are this high. All he knows is that if Ryan's going to stay like this, Avery's not going to stay in Kindling much longer. He knows this is a shame, but also knows it's true.

"Please," he says. To Ryan. To the universe.

Ryan knocks the back of his head into the passenger seat's headrest. Then he turns and looks Avery in the eye.

"I'm sorry," he says. "Truly, I'm sorry. I'm such a dick."

"It's okay. We haven't passed the point of no return."

Ryan shakes his head. "Yeah, but I almost put us there, didn't I?" His phone buzzes in his pocket, and he takes it out. When he sees the screen, he laughs. He shows it to Avery—a text from Alicia.

You're fucking this up, boy. Don't be a dick.

"Guess she liked you," Ryan says.

"I liked her," Avery says. "All of them."

"Even Dez?"

"Eighty percent."

Ryan nods. "Sounds about right. And where did I stand, two minutes ago?"

"Forty percent? Thirty-seven?"

"So what should we do? I want to get back up into the nineties."

What do you want to do?

I don't know—what do you want to do?

This time, Avery answers.

"Let's go get your aunt's boat," he says. "I want to head back to the water."

It's not that Ryan has forgotten. And he certainly hasn't forgiven. But he's remembered: He only has another year of this. Skylar and his friends will never leave. But Ryan will get away. Even if it's as simple as stealing away with a pink-haired boy.

Meanwhile, Harry can't hold it in anymore. He just can't. His body makes up his mind for him, and right there, right in front of everyone else, he is peeing himself. Once it starts it's almost impossible to stop. In horror, he feels his underwear grow wet. The front of his jeans.

* * *

Craig feels Harry tense, doesn't know what's going on. Neither one of them can really see down, not the way they're standing. Harry spells out an *S*, then an *O*, *R*, *R*, and *Y* on Craig's back. Craig responds with a question mark. Then Harry responds with a *P*, and instead of being disgusted, Craig snorts out a laugh.

Smita notices, but nobody else does. Harry wouldn't even know that she knows, but she walks over and adjusts the fan so it's blowing lower, right onto his pants.

An hour left. All they want is for there to be an hour left. And then there is only an hour left.

The sun is dropping from the sky, taking a little of the day's warmth with it. The local news stations are beaming their reports to the national news. Tonight, late-night talk-show hosts will talk about two boys kissing. Radio switchboards will light up. Fox News will ignore it, then decry it. Wherever he is, Craig's father will make sure the televisions and radios stay off, the computers unconnected from the wider world.

He doesn't want his other sons to see.

* * *

Harry doesn't want to drink any more water, any more energy drinks. As a result, he feels light-headed. Unbelievable as it may seem, there are moments when he barely knows where he is. He slaps himself on the chest to keep awake.

Cooper approaches a big bridge that spans a big river, with a big city on the other side. When we were growing up, this scene was what we always envisioned as the opening credits of our new life. Even those of us born in the city imagined this. Whether we were driving ourselves or in the back of a yellow cab, the city would spread out in its infinite wonder, each window glittering with invitation, the skyscrapers pointing like arrows to the heights we might attain. For most of us, it didn't play out as easily, but there was still the thrill of those opening credits that carried us through the harder times, that sustained our faith in a city that often didn't show much faith in us. Even as we were dying, we'd remember that first arrival, or we would remember how we'd pictured how the arrival would be, or we would conflate the two things—the memory, the dream—into one reality, and that would seem to us like a long time ago, but still a time worth visiting.

As Cooper nears the city, we can't help but feel a little of that excitement, a little recognition of the escapes we made, of the finish line we crossed, only to find so many other finish lines waiting after it.

We watch Cooper's car in the parade of headlights. All those cars. All those pilgrims. But Cooper's car breaks free. His headlights change direction. We watch as he pulls out of the toll lane, narrows onto the local roads. Right under the bridge, right near the joint where it juts from the land and into the air, he pulls over. Turns off the ignition. Steps out of the car.

He's parked illegally and doesn't care. The sign right there says NO PARKING AT ANY TIME. He shuts the car door without locking it. Then, without looking back, he heads for the bridge. We peer in and see his wallet on the passenger seat. The phone charger. Some receipts and change. He's left everything behind, except for his phone, which he's taken with him.

Our first reaction is, *Don't leave your wallet in an unlocked car*.

Then we step back. We have to step back. We have to stop thinking about the city, remembering the city. We have to focus. Up until this moment, there was room to believe he was heading in another direction. But now there's only one direction.

We yell at him, yell after him. Even though we no longer have voices, we scream at the top of our lungs. We crowd ourselves into a mangled chorus, and in anguish we hear the nothing that comes from our lips. We try to block him, and he walks right through us. We try to pound on his car, raise an alarm, but we can't do anything.

Cars pass by. He is, to them, just another teenage boy. Out for a walk. Crossing the bridge. They see him throw something into the river. They don't realize it's his phone.

We try to catch it. We cannot catch it.

He feels the railing under his hands. No. The railing is under his hands, but he doesn't really feel it. He walks toward the center of the bridge. It will take him about two minutes to get there. Maybe three. He's in no rush. He watches the dark water undulating far below.

He cannot see his mother crying in her bedroom. No matter what his father says, she will not let go of her phone.

We howl at him. Beg with him. Plead with him. Yell at him. Explain to him. Our lives were short, and we never would have wanted to have them be shorter. Sometimes perspective comes far too late. You cannot trust yourself. You think you can, but you can't. Not because you are selfish. You cannot live for anyone else's sake. As much as you may want to, you can't stay alive just because other people want you alive. You cannot stay alive for your parents. You cannot stay alive for your friends. And you have no responsibility to stay alive for them. You have no responsibility to anyone but yourself to live.

But I'm dead, he would tell us. *I am already dead.*

No, we'd argue. *No, you are not.* We know what it is like to be alive in the present but dead in the future. But you are the opposite. Your future self is still alive. You have a responsibility to your future self, who is someone you might not even know, might not even understand yet. Because until you die, that future self has as much of a life as you do.

We can see that future self. Even if you can't. We can see him. He is made up not just of your present soul, but of all our souls, all our possibilities, all our deaths. He is the opposite of our negation.

You are not worthless, we shout to Cooper. Your life is not disposable.

You think there is no point.

You think you will never find a place.

You think your pain is the only emotion you will ever feel. You think nothing else will ever come close to being as strong as that pain.

You are certain of this.

In this minute—in this, the most important minute of your life—you are certain that you must die.

You see no other option.

You need to wake up, we cry.

Listen to us. We fruitlessly demand that you listen to us. We shit blood and had our skin lacerated and broken by lesions. We had fungus grow in our throats, under our fingernails. We lost the ability to see, to speak, to feed ourselves. We coughed up pieces of ourselves and felt our blood turn to magma. We lost the use of our muscles and our bodies were reduced to collections of skin-encased bones. We were rendered unrecognizable, diminished and demolished. Our lovers had to watch us die. Our friends had to watch as the nurse changed our catheters, had to try to put aside that image as they laid us in caskets, into the ground. We will never kiss our mothers again. We will never see our fathers. We will never feel air in our lungs. We will never hear the sound of our voices. We will never feel snow or sand or take part in another conversation. Everything was taken away from us, and we miss it. We miss all of it. Even if you cannot feel it now, it is all there for you.

Cooper is nearing the center of the bridge. Cars continue to pulse past him; when a truck rolls by, he can feel the bridge shake, can feel the air displaced. This he feels. Even if he has closed himself into his decision, he is still in the world.

The last minute.

The last thirty seconds.

Our ends were never this precise.

We want to close our eyes. Why can't we close our eyes? We who did nothing more than dream and love and screw—why have we been banished here, why hasn't the world solved this by now? Why must we watch as Cooper steps up to the railing? Why must we watch as a twelve-year-old puts a gun to his head and pulls the trigger? Why must we watch as a fourteen-year-old hangs himself in the garage, to be found by his grandmother two hours later? Why must we watch as a nineteen-year-old is strung up on the side of an empty highway and left to die? Why must we watch as a thirteen-year-old takes a stomach full of pills, then places a plastic bag over his head? Why must we watch as he vomits and chokes?

Why must we die over and over again?

Cooper lifts himself into the air. Here we are, thousands of us, shouting no, shouting at him to stop, crying out and making a net of our bodies, trying to come between him and the water, even though we know—we always know—that no matter how tight a net we make, no matter how hard we try, he will still fall through.

We die over and over again.

Over and over again.

Cooper jumps onto the railing and he is slammed from the side. Before he can know what's happening, before we can know what's happening, he's being brought back to the ground, tackled to the ground. He cries out, but the cry is ignored. A driver, seeing what's happening, screeches to a halt, and the car behind almost hits him. Cooper is struggling, Cooper is trying to get back up, but the man on top of him is telling him not to move, to stay still, to stay there. Cooper feels the man holding him, feels the man not letting go. They get a good look at each other at the same time. Cooper sees a uniform, a badge—a traffic cop. The cop sees Cooper and says, "Jesus, you're just a kid."

Other people are running over, are asking what's wrong, are asking the cop if he needs help. Cooper starts to shake, all of his emotions bursting out at once. Anger and sadness at having been stopped. Humiliation. Self-loathing—he couldn't even do this right. And somewhere in there, a small voice of relief.

The cop is still holding the wallet he found in the car. Not letting go of Cooper, he hands the wallet to the concerned woman next to him and asks her to tell him the boy's name. She does, and then the cop lets some of his weight off Cooper and turns him, so he can look the boy in the eye.

"It might not feel like it," the cop says, "but, Cooper, today is your lucky day."

It does not bring back the twelve-year-old who put a gun to his head. It does not bring back the fourteen-year-old who hung himself. It does not bring back the nineteen-year-old strung up on the side of an empty highway and left to die. It does not bring back the thirteen-year-old who took a stomach full of pills. It does not bring back any of us.

But it does bring back Cooper.

* * *

190

Less than an hour's drive away, Craig and Harry reach their final hour, as Neil and Peter watch from the crowd.

Craig feels strangely awake, immensely alive. His body is sore, his mind is overwhelmed, and the air smells like sweat and pee, but after thirty-one hours he can't see himself or Harry dropping before they hit thirty-two hours, twelve minutes, and ten seconds. He's even allowing himself to take in the crowd, to wave to the people who are cheering and to all of the cameras that have gathered.

Harry, however, feels like his body is about to fail. He can't bear the thought of another minute of this. In some twisted way, we know how he feels. When our bodies were failing, we'd often feel like the space between breaths was centuries long. And then sleep would be over in a blink, leaving us more exhausted than ever.

He's tried shaking his legs, moving his legs. Doing the small workouts they'd planned. But this is it. He can't anymore. He can't imagine disappointing all these people, can't imagine disappointing his parents and, most of all, Craig. But he can't imagine fifty-six more minutes of this. He's trying to think of a way to communicate this to Craig. He's trying to think of a way to ask forgiveness before he lets go. He needs a break. He needs something.

Out of desperation, he wraps his arms around Craig, pulls him closer, pulls him tight. Craig does the same thing. First, just an embrace. A hug. Then squeezing. Harder and harder. With all the energy they have left.

Only there's more energy after that, too. Because he's still standing. He's still holding on. He's not letting go. Neither of them is letting go. They're making it more intense. Runners sprinting at the end of the marathon. Despite the exhaustion, there's the need to see it through.

The crowd in the back cheers louder. The people in front have a different reaction. Tariq is near tears, because he can see the pain his friends are in, can see them struggling. Mr. and Mrs. Ramirez must fight off the instinct they have to keep Harry safe, to protect him from any pain. Smita worries about what will happen if they don't make it, how they will deal with that kind of failure. Sure, people will say it's amazing they lasted this long. But it will still be a failure.

Harry doesn't have to write any letters on Craig's back for Craig to know he's going to have to hold tight for the remaining time they have. This is now the way things are. So Craig holds tight. And as he does, he tries to take in all of the sensations, all of the things he is seeing and feeling and hearing. Nothing like this will ever happen to him again, and he wants to remember it. And nothing like this will ever happen with him and Harry again, a fact that he is trying to place in the context of his love for Harry. Now that they've shared this, it would be natural to want to try again. And part of Craig *does* want to try again, wants to see if there's any way to carry some of this intensity over into their real lives. But he's also remembering what Harry said to him when they were breaking up, how they would still be important to each other, and that was the important thing. Craig hadn't wanted to hear it then, and he wouldn't really want it repeated now. But he also knows it's true.

So now he's back to the question of why he's done this crazy thing. From all the camera crews, he knows the story is going to spread, and he hopes that maybe it'll make people a little less scared of two boys kissing than they were before, and a little more welcoming to the idea that all people are, in fact, born equal, no matter who they kiss or screw, no matter what dreams they have or love they give. So there's that. But that's not a personal reason. What is his personal reason? If it's not getting back together with Harry. If it's not making his family see who he is, and having them cheering him on.

What Craig finds when he takes all of these people out of the equation is the single variable of himself. He realizes: He is doing it for himself. Not for glory. Not for popularity. Not even for admiration. He is doing it because he feels alive. There are so many minutes and hours and days we spend taking life for granted, not feeling it so much as going along with it. But then there are moments like this, when the aliveness of life is crystalline, palpable, undeniable. It is the ultimate buoy against drowning. It is the ever-saving grace.

Forty-two. Thirty-four. Twenty-six! The crowd calls out numbers on minute-wide intervals. They filter around Harry like the temperature, but he has to stay focused on the kiss, on making sure his lips stay on Craig's. He is sure that if Craig lets go of him, he will fall to the ground.

Twenty-two! Nineteen!

A car pulls up to the side of the George Washington Bridge, and Cooper's parents come running out. They find their son sitting in a security booth, a traffic cop at his side, allowing him his silence. It should not be the case, but at that moment, they have never loved him more.

Seventeen! Sixteen!

Merrily, merrily, a blue-haired boy and a pink-haired boy

row on a quiet river, serenaded by their own conversation. This is now their place. They will return here many times.

Thirteen! Twelve!

We wish we could have been there for you. We didn't have many role models of our own—we latched on to the foolish love of Oscar Wilde and the well-versed longing of Walt Whitman because nobody else was there to show us an untortured path. We were going to be your role models. We were going to give you art and music and confidence and shelter and a much better world. Those who survived lived to do this. But we haven't been there for you. We've been here. Watching as you become the role models.

Ten! Nine!

Neil and Peter call out the numbers along with everyone else. They hold hands, feel like they are witnessing something monumental, something that could change things. It won't, but that feeling, that spirit will live on in everyone here, everyone who sees. The spirit will change things.

Eight! Seven! Six!

Tariq sees that there are almost half a million people, around the world, who are watching this. Then he stops looking at the computer and looks straight at life.

Five! Four!

We're going to do this, Harry thinks.

Three! Two!

I am alive, Craig thinks.

One.

We watch you, but we can't intervene. We have already done our part. Just as you are doing your part, whether you know it or not, whether you mean to or not, whether you want to or not.

Choose your actions wisely.

There will come a time—perhaps even by the time you read this—that people will no longer be on Facebook. There will come a time when the stars of your favorite teen TV show will be sixty. There will come a time when you will have the same unalienable rights as your straightest friend. (Probably before any of the stars of your favorite teen TV show turn sixty.) There will come a time when the gay prom won't have to be separate. There will come a time when you will look at someone younger than you and feel that he or she will know more than you ever did. There will come a time when you will worry about being forgotten. There will come a time when the gospel will be rewritten.

If you play your cards right, the next generation will have so much more than you did.

Cooper will live to meet his future self.

You should all live to meet your future selves.

* * *

We saw our friends die. But we also see our friends live. So many of them live, and we often toast their long and full lives. They carry us on.

There is the sudden. There is the eventual.
And in between, there is the living.

We do not start as dust. We do not end as dust. We make more than dust.

That's all we ask of you. Make more than dust.

Author's Note and Acknowledgments

On September 18, 2010, college students Matty Daley and Bobby Canciello kissed for thirty-two hours, thirty minutes, and forty-seven seconds (longer than the characters in this book) to break the Guinness World Record for longest continuous kiss. I am just one of many people who were inspired by what they did. While the characters in this book are not in any way based on Matty and Bobby, the story is certainly inspired by what they did. I am grateful to Matty for telling me what it was like, and for continuing to inspire.

On September 22, 2010, four days after Matty and Bobby's kiss, another student named Tyler Clementi killed himself by jumping off the George Washington Bridge. He went to a college about a half hour away from Matty and Bobby. While this juxtaposition certainly informed this novel, I want to be clear that with the exception of the bridge, none of the circumstances of what happened to Tyler Clementi are meant to be portrayed in this book. That is his own story, and one that I would never presume to know.

At some point in 2008, Michael Cart asked me to be a part of a new anthology he was putting together. He was gathering authors to write about LGBT life today, and as soon as I said yes (which was a foregone conclusion—I would write just about anything for Michael Cart), I felt the challenge of the assignment. In the end, I decided to write a story about the generation of gay men that went before me looking at the generation of gay men that came after me. (My gay "generation" is a very short one—I came of age in the five or six years that existed between the height of the AIDS epidemic and the proliferation of the Internet, the former defining the generation before me, and the latter defining the generation after me.) The voice of this book and its first few pages began as that story, in the anthology that would ultimately be titled *How Beautiful the Ordinary*. This novel would not exist if Michael hadn't asked me to write the story. He has been such a gracious advocate for my writing over the years, and now I have one more reason to be grateful for him.

While I was in college in the 1990s, my uncle Bobby came extraordinarily close to dying from AIDS. Now, twenty years later, I can stand on Broadway with my best friends, and a stylish, smiling man will breeze by on his Segway, on his way to work, and one of my best friends will say, "Look, it's Uncle Bobby!" Bobby has already written some of his story—when you do the Google search, call him Robert Levithan, not Bobby—and I have no doubt he will write much more of it in the near future. I very much look forward to reading it.

On November 12, 2010, my best friend, Billy Merrell, legally married his already-husband, Nico Medina, in the District of Columbia. After the ceremony, the wedding party went to see HIDE/SEEK, the first ever queer-and-billed-as-queer exhibit in the history of the Smithsonian. One of the paintings in the exhibit was David Hockney's *We Two Boys Together Clinging*. The title, as the placard next to the painting explained, came from a Walt Whitman poem. I immediately thought of Matty and Bobby's kiss—so much so that I later remembered the phrase as "We Two Boys Kissing," which became the inspiration for the title of this book. A misremembering of Whitman filtered through Hockney, a wedding day, and a thirty-two-hour kiss . . . I am often asked where my ideas come from, and this is a pretty good representation of what the answer might look like.

In 2012, while I was working on this book, I did something that I'd never done before: I read it to someone out loud as it was still coming together. That someone was Joel Pavelski, and those readings took place in many fine public spaces in the city of New York, with a finale overlooking the Pacific Ocean. Thank you for listening, Joel. And thanks as well to Nick Eliopulos and David Barrett Graver, who both gave meaningful feedback on the book when it was still in manuscript form; to Melina Marchetta, who was the exact right dinner companion to have on the day I most needed to talk about my ending; and to Libba Bray, for being Libba Bray.

My editor, Nancy Hinkel, is a better reason to jump for joy than a pretty boy in his underwear . . . and that is, as Stephin Merritt knows, saying a lot. I have, as of this writing, ten years of thankfulness for her and for the whole team at Random House, including (but in no way limited to) Lauren Donovan, Isabel Warren-Lynch, Stephen Brown, Adrienne Waintraub, Tracy Lerner, and Lisa Nadel. I am also thankful for the efforts of Bill Clegg, Alicia Gordon, Shaun Dolan, and everyone at WMEE. Thanks to Evan Walsh for perfectly capturing the book with his cover photograph.

This isn't a book that I could have written ten years ago.

And as much as I'd love to credit that to my growth as a writer, I know it's not really that. Instead it's because of all the people I've met and talked to as an author. And, just as important, it's about all of the things I've been exposed to as a reader, particularly of YA fiction. I am so lucky to be a part of a community of writers that constantly inspires me to write whatever I want to write, no matter how hard it seems. My peers are my role models, and my role models are my peers. Which is extraordinary.

Thanks as always to my parents, my family, my friends, and my readers.

Finally, thank you to all the role models I never got to meet.

For more information and a list of books that inspired and informed this novel, go to davidlevithan.com/twoboyskissing.

About the Author

David Levithan is the author of many acclaimed novels, some of them solo works, some of them collaborations. His solo novels include the *New York Times* bestselling *Every Day, Boy Meets Boy, The Realm of Possibility, Are We There Yet?, Wide Awake, Love Is the Higher Law,* and *The Lover's Dictionary.* His collaborations include *Will Grayson, Will Grayson* (written with John Green), *Marly's Ghost* (illustrated by Brian Selznick), and *Every You, Every Me* (with photographs by Jonathan Farmer), as well as three novels written with Rachel Cohn: *Nick & Norah's Infinite Playlist, Naomi and Ely's No Kiss List,* and *Dash & Lily's Book of Dares.* He lives in Hoboken, New Jersey, and spends his days in New York City, editing and publishing other people's books.